A
Cry of Angry Thunder

A
Cry of Angry Thunder

G. CLIFTON WISLER

DOUBLEDAY & COMPANY, INC.

GARDEN CITY, NEW YORK

1980

All of the characters in this book are fictitious, and any resemblance to actual persons, living or dead, except for historical personages, is purely coincidental.

ISBN: 0-385-15657-X
Library of Congress Catalog Card Number 79-7885
Copyright © 1980 by G. Clifton Wisler
First Edition
Printed in the United States of America

for my parents

A
Cry of Angry Thunder

CHAPTER 1

The West has a charm, a beauty all its own. It is not a land of gleaming splendor or sparkling lakes. It is a hostile land, a hard land where the blazing sun and the biting cold eat away at a man's soul. But to those who belong to the broad grass-lands and barren hills, the land fills their hearts with the warmth one can only feel when looking upon the landscapes of home.

I felt that warmth now, even though there was a chill in the September air. The grass beneath my feet burned yellow in the sunlight, and I watched the familiar outline of the Lara-mie Mountains reflected in the still waters of the North Platte River.

My destination was close at hand, but I halted my journey for a time, eager to drink in the familiar sights. As the huge yellow sun settled into the mist of the mountains, my mind was flooded with memories. As I rode across the valley where I'd killed my first buffalo, I failed to see the scattered farms that lined the river. I overlooked the thin wisps of smoke that curled upward from the chimneys of the farmhouses. Like-wise the sounds of barking dogs and screaming children failed to penetrate my ears.

Civilization had come to the North Platte in my absence. The hills no longer echoed with the shouts of Indian hunting parties. I saw no long trains of canvas-covered wagons thun-dering their way westward. No buckskin-clad traders sat across twilight campfires from weathered red-faced chiefs dressed in eagle feathers and bear claws.

A time had passed for the North Platte. For me, also. Life

would be different in the days ahead. I found myself missing the other days, those left so long ago and far away. I also found myself fearing the uncertainty of an unknown future. That much, at least, I had in common with that other time so many years before when I'd first entered the broad valley of the North Platte.

It was autumn that year, too, but everything else was different. The weather was cold, chilling my small ten-year-old bones. I huddled against the side of the big freight wagon, wishing I'd ridden in the back of the cook wagon with my mother. But I was a man, more or less, and my father would have expected me to ride up front in a supply wagon like the soldier he always assumed I'd become.

My father was a wonderful man, full of splendid stories. He was a hard man, toughened by the wars that had made him old and weary. But I was his only son, and he always had a softness, a warmth for me which he shielded from everyone else except my mother.

Father was a soldier, first, last, and always. He'd fought at Vera Cruz and Mexico City, rising to the rank of captain before returning home.

Father married my mother in 1851, and I came into the world two years later. For a time we lived in little army posts from Texas to Massachusetts. Then the southern states went to war with Mr. Lincoln, and Father took us to his mother's house in York, Pennsylvania. Then Father rode off to battle.

Grandmother Whitlock was an austere old woman in her middle sixties. She had no patience for the scampering eight-year-old I had become, and I cried myself to sleep many nights hoping the war would be a short one and Father would return.

For Father, the war *was* short. Promoted to colonel, he led a charge at the battle for Manassas Junction. Some rebel rifleman planted a minnie ball in his shoulder, and he died three days later in Washington.

We buried him in the family cemetery behind Grandmother Whitlock's big house. Mother never smiled after that, and I was lost. Grandmother hollered and screamed all the time, and I cried more and more. Then one night Mother visited my small room and sat down beside me on the huge bed that had been my father's before it was mine.

"Johnny, why are you crying?" she asked.

"I'm not crying," I said, swallowing my tears. "Soldiers don't cry."

"Sometimes they do," Mother told me. "Especially if they aren't too big. I think even soldiers cry when they hurt."

"Father said soldiers never cry. They're tough. You have to be very brave to be a soldier."

"Johnny, I don't think your father would mind you crying for him. He would have cried for you. He loved you very much."

"Then why'd he go away?" I asked.

"Don't you know?" Mother asked me. "He talked to you often about it. You remember all those medals you always admired. What you admired was the courage that earned them. A brave man can't run away from a battle. He leads. But the thing you must always remember is that your father fought to protect you and me. In a way, he sacrificed himself for us."

I leaned against her warm womanly body, stretching my small arms around her.

"I've missed this part of you, Johnny," she said. "You got to be a young man almost before I knew it. You should have some more years as a boy yet, but I'm afraid life hasn't given you many of those."

"I don't understand," I said.

"Well, look at it like this. You're already the man of the house. Your grandmother and I need you to be our man, to take care of us."

"No one needs to take care of Grandmother," I said. "She's fierce. I'd rather face a full rebel brigade than Grandmother."

"Your father told you some wonderful stories, Johnny. Never forget them."

"I won't," I told my mother. "There won't be any others."

I really believed that when I finally squirmed beneath the

quilts on that cold Pennsylvania night. I believed there would never again be a hard man with a tender side just for me. I believed I was sentenced to a life full of harsh words from my grandmother and lonely nights of crying for my father.

All that changed about three weeks later. Grandmother Whitlock simply didn't have the disposition needed to tolerate a child in the house. She arranged for me to be sent to a small military academy in Philadelphia, but Mother objected.

"That boy's too small to be a man," Mother argued. "I won't have him made into a soldier, too."

"Well, he most certainly cannot stay in this house," Grandmother said. "He must be schooled properly."

"There are many kinds of schooling, Mrs. Whitlock," Mother said. "I will wire my father. We will go to join him."

Mother was never a strong person. I'd never known her to argue with Father or anyone. But she was like a tempest that night. Nothing could sway her. She received an answer to her telegram two days later, and when spring came, we were heading westward on the railroad.

I was not yet eleven years old, and I don't remember the path we took. I do remember we joined up with an army relief detachment somewhere in Kansas, and I made the long journey to Fort Laramie on the front seat of a supply wagon next to a bearded old sergeant named O'Brien.

The trip was a long one. I was frail for someone who was supposed to be a man, and it wore me down. My eastern upbringing never prepared me for the long days of dust and thirst. I was a pitiful thing, my seventy pounds hiding under a grimy face and long blond hair. The blue eyes which had flashed with mischief at Grandmother Whitlock's house were mainly filled with sleeplessness and fatigue.

I learned more about the Army on that trip than a thousand of my father's stories could have taught me. The men were not brave warriors at all. Most of them were simple men who were soldiers because it was all they knew how to do.

I found myself feeling sorry for some of them, and I began to understand myself a little better. My desire to be a soldier, a hero like my father, didn't include the weary camp life these men endured. For the first time, I realized, too, that it never included the idea of dying in battle as Father had.

On the quieter evenings when the trail had been easy on us, Mother would tell me of the land which lay ahead to the west. Rich valleys, seas of yellow grass, mountains which stretched to the sky. But most of all, she spoke of her father, the famous Trader Jim Howard.

Each time she spoke of him, Sergeant O'Brien would add some story of his own. If my grandfather was half as tall, half as strong, half as brave as they said, he would be the fiercest man in creation.

Mother told me he lived at Fort Laramie in the Dakota Territory now. He traded goods to the Indians for blankets and hides. It didn't seem like much of a life to me, but Mother said it suited him.

"When I was a little girl, Johnny, your grandfather was a great man. There weren't many white men around, just Sioux and Cheyenne and Arapaho. Shoshoni and Blackfeet to the west, Crow and Arikara to the north."

"Indians?" I asked.

"Yes," she said. "After my mother died, Papa took a Cheyenne woman for his wife. She lived with us for almost ten years. Then she caught the smallpox from some people on a wagon train and died."

"I'll bet he's killed a lot of Indians," I said.

"He's killed a lot of game," she said. "He's never killed any man he didn't have to kill. He's had to kill a few Indians and a few whites in his time, but he stands high with the tribes. The Sioux honor him, and they honor few white men."

"I guess he's been everywhere," I said.

"In his younger days, he trapped beaver all the way up in Oregon. He's guided a few wagons down the Humboldt cutoff into California. But mainly he just trades with the Indians and hunts in the Platte and Powder River valleys."

"Powder River," I said. "That sounds like a western river.

Words like powder and blood and snake make good names for rivers."

"Maybe if you grow to like your grandfather, he'll take you north to see the Missouri. It's a great river. He took me once when he was taking trade goods to a Crow village. I was just a girl then, but I'll never forget the way those Indians looked at him. He's such a big man, and they think of him as a great warrior."

"Even though he's not a soldier?" I asked.

"The Indians don't care much for our soldiers," she explained. "The soldiers shoot and kill Indians with very little reason. The early trappers and hunters understood the Indians. The Indians knew they could trust the old-timers. But the men who come now cause problems, bring war."

"Then they won't trust me," I sighed.

"They will, Johnny," she said, taking my small hand in hers. "You'll grow to know life as your grandfather does. You'll learn the streams and the mountains in a way I never could."

"You never could?" I asked.

"I never could," she said. "Papa never had much use for a girl. The Indians trade off their daughters. Papa sent me off to live with his brother in Tennessee."

"Is that where you met Father?" I asked.

"Yes."

"Then why come back here?" I asked. "You always liked it in Pennsylvania."

"For you, Johnny," she said, smiling at me with a special brightness in her eyes I'd not seen in months.

"For me?" I asked, confused.

"Your grandfather will help you grow into the kind of man your father would have wanted you to be," she said. "Back in Philadelphia you would have turned into one of those eastern dandies your father always despised."

"Grandfather must be something," I said, trying to imagine what the old frontiersman would look like.

"You'll know very soon," she said.

That night visions of my grandfather danced through my

dreams. He would be a huge man, taller than my father. I imagined him dressed in a great buffalo coat, an enormous rifle in his hands. He would have a long white beard and piercing eyes.

I dreamed of the two of us riding Indian ponies across the plains, killing buffalo and fighting Indians. I saved his life and he saved mine. I stood small beside him, but my face bore great courage. I was stronger than a bear and braver than any Sioux who'd ever lived.

It was all fantasy, of course. I was too small, too frail, too weak to fight anyone or anything. But it is the way of youth to dream, so I could do no other thing.

My very real fears that my grandfather would find me too weak and too small were kept away by my dream. In my dream, he was never disappointed in me. And so while in the power of that beautiful world of dreams and adventures, I set aside my cares and slept peacefully.

CHAPTER 2

We were on the trail most of the morning. It was the same as always before, our small train of wagons snaking its way across the broad flatlands beside the Platte. It was warmer than usual, and the wind which had become so familiar to me seemed to have died away in the morning sunlight. Sergeant O'Brien whistled softly some old Irish folk ballad his mother had taught him. I usually tried to pick up the melody and hum along with him, but I was too nervous that morning. I just sat quietly, searching the horizon for some sign of the fort.

When the sun had climbed high in the sky, I saw at last something rising from the prairie grasses.

"Is that it?" I asked O'Brien, pointing with my skinny arm at the spot.

"Laramie? Sure is, my boy," O'Brien said. "Brave little fort all alone in the heart of Cheyenne and Sioux country."

"I don't see any Indians," I said.

"You will, boy," he told me.

I leaned back against the canvas supports, trying my best to reinforce my fading courage.

"You think the Indians will attack?" I asked.

"Indians ain't at war now. We's the only ones at war. They probably bustin' their guts laughin' at the stupid white men fightin' each other in the lands beyond the mighty waters."

"Have you been to Laramie before?" I asked O'Brien.

"Spent close to seven years out here. Fought Cheyennes and Sioux, Pawnee and Kiowa. I had myself three arrows in me. But this here's my last trip out here. I got to pick up the regulars and take 'em back to fight the rebels."

"Won't that mean the Indians will attack?"

"No, boy," O'Brien told me, slapping me on the back. "It most likely means things'll be nice and peaceful out here for a few years. Most Indians do just fine when the settlers leave 'em be. Won't be too many trains headin' for Oregon and California. This is goin' to be a mighty nice place to be for a while."

"What are the Indians really like, Sergeant O'Brien? Are they big and ugly and savage? That's what I've heard."

"I could tell you, boy, but I won't. I tell you this secret, and you remember it. It's always best to make up your own mind about people and things. You let other people decide things for you, there's no reason for you to be around."

I asked no more questions of O'Brien. As we neared the fort, my answers came quickly. The Platte seemed to broaden somewhat there, and the fort was not far distant. It was a military post, and soldiers rode out to meet us.

For a minute I fixed my eyes on the column of soldiers riding beside our wagons. They all looked terribly young to me. They lacked the beards of my father's regiment. They reminded me of the wooden soldiers I'd had to leave behind in York. Each one of the men was spotlessly dressed in blue with bright silver buttons on their shirts. They carried long sabers at their sides, and their white gloves and neckerchiefs seemed to me to belong better in a picture book back East than on horses riding across the plains.

I didn't spend many moments gazing at the soldiers. My curiosity was reserved for the fort itself. It was made up of lines of stone buildings huddled around a parade ground. The proud flag I knew so well flew from a tall staff in the center of the fort.

Between the fort and the Laramie River a miniature city of tents sprang up in neat rows to house the soldiers. Opposite the army tents were clusters of tepees housing Sioux, Cheyenne, and Arapaho Indians. I was amazed to find the Indians dressed in warm buffalo hides and bearskins. I'd always pictured them half naked and wild-eyed. They seemed perfectly at home in the company of soldiers, and I spotted no weapons on them.

O'Brien pointed out the various buildings of importance as we rode into the fort. Then he pulled the wagon up to the supply warehouse, and I jumped down.

"You take care of that hide of yours, boy," O'Brien said, smiling broadly with his Irish grin. Then he returned to his duties, and I ran to find Mother. I looked in every direction for her, but my eyes couldn't locate a sign of her. Then I caught a glimpse of her white Philadelphia-bought dress. She was standing beside three army officers, and I ran to her.

"Mother," I said, tugging at her arm. "When will I meet Grandfather?"

"Excuse him, gentlemen," she said, pulling me in front of her. "This is my son, John. He's a trifle wild after the long trip from the East."

"Hello, John," a tall man with a heavy black mustache said. "I'm Major Kincaid, deputy post commander. Welcome to Fort Laramie."

"Thank you, sir," I said, coming to stiff attention and giving him a crisp salute. "I'm pleased to meet you."

"At ease, John," the major said, returning my salute. "I'd like you to meet Lieutenants Allen and French."

I saluted them, too, and they tried not to smile as they saluted back.

"My father was a soldier," I said. "He was a colonel."

"They know, Johnny," Mother said, holding me against her. "Major Kincaid served with your father in Mexico."

"You knew Father?" I asked the major.

"He was a fine officer and a fine man," the major told me. "I was sad to hear he was killed."

"He was leading a charge at Manassas," I said. "He died bravely." Inside I was wishing for the first time that he'd not been such a brave man.

"A man does what he has to do, John," Major Kincaid said.

"To win a war, someone has to lead the charge. You never heard of a victory won without someone dying. It's hard on those who are left behind, but death is as much a part of life as birth."

"Yes, sir," I said.

"Why so sad?" Mother asked me. "You're about to meet your very famous grandfather. Well?" she asked, walking away. "Are you coming?"

"Yes," I said, scampering behind her.

Mother led the way down the dusty street. In all the time I'd known her, I'd never seen her so powerful, so sure of herself. Perhaps it was being out West that made the difference. Eastern women were more reserved, more timid. But every woman I saw out West seemed to walk with purpose.

Mother stopped when she came to a small wooden building with a small house behind it. There was a sign over the door which read "Howard Trading Post and Dry Goods Store." I followed Mother inside.

Two Indians stood at the end of a long wooden counter, bargaining with a white-haired man over the price of rifle ammunition. Mother pushed me over to the counter, then turned to face the old man.

The store was suddenly filled with silence. Then the old man leaped across the room and hugged my mother.

"Dear God, but you've made a handsome woman," he said. "I never thought you'd make it when you were such a little bird of a girl. Why, you did me proud."

He turned to the Indians and said something to them in their language. They smiled and answered him.

"Even the Sioux agree you're a fine woman. Old Many Blankets here says you'd bring five horses even as a woman of age," Grandfather said.

"Well," Mother said, frowning, "you tell old Many Blankets he can just keep his horses."

Grandfather laughed so loud that the room shook. Then he turned toward me and froze.

"Is this the boy?" he asked. "Is this young Johnny?"

"Yes, sir," I said. "I'm pleased to meet you."

"What kind of talk is this?" he asked, turning to Mother. "Mary, did you teach this boy to talk like this?"

"He's an Easterner," she explained. "He's grown up on army posts and in fine houses. The last few years he's been around his grandmother and her Philadelphia friends."

"A grandson of mine," he said, shaking his head.

I watched as he examined me from head to toe. I could tell he wasn't pleased. I was too weak, too frail, too eastern for his taste.

"Are you a boy?" he asked me at last.

"Not any longer," I told him, managing a tough stare. "When my father died, I became a man. I have a mother to take care of."

"You could hardly take care of a woman," he said, laughing.

"I may be thin and talk different than you're used to, but I'm not as weak as you might think. I can fire a rifle, and I know the manual of arms from cover to cover. I'll be eleven years old in a few weeks," I told him, staring intently.

"Papa, please," Mother said. "I brought him out here two thousand miles so he'd have a father. I didn't bring him out here for you to mistreat him."

"What do you say to that, boy?" he asked. "Does your mother fight your battles?"

"My father was a soldier," I said. "He faced death many times, but he never turned away from the face of battle. He told me that. He said a man who walks away from danger isn't a man at all. Test me," I said, stepping forward. "Hit me. I won't cry. I'll get stronger, bigger."

He walked over to me and took out a huge knife from a sheath on his belt. He held it up against my face, smiling a vicious smile. I stared at him with a stiff lip, never flinching. Then he set the knife down and smiled broadly.

"You got grit to you, boy," he said, taking me in his two huge hands. "You'd have made a mountain man."

As he lifted me off the ground, I felt the great power in his arms. He was much stronger than I'd ever have thought. His white hair had misled me into thinking he was soft in the way old men are in the East. He was solid as a rock, though, and tough as an old bear.

"I'll try not to disappoint you," I said as he set me down.

"As long as you look every man dead level in his eyes, never tell no lies, never shirk your work, you'll never bring shame on this family. You ever do bring shame, you'll answer for it to Trader Jim Howard."

"Yes, sir," I said to him.

"Now come meet some friends of mine," he said, leading me past my mother.

"Many Blankets," Grandfather said, "this is my grandson, Johnny. We must find a Sioux name for him, but for now, we'll call him Johnny."

The tall Indian named Many Blankets spoke to the other Indian at his side. Then they looked at me.

"Boy, this man is Painted Bow, a great warrior of the Oglala Sioux. He speaks no English, but he is a very powerful man. He honors you with his presence."

"What do I do?" I asked.

"Smile at him, boy," Grandfather said.

I turned to the Indian and forced a smile onto my face. He grinned at me, searching my face for something. Then he took me in his hands and clasped me to his chest. I squirmed a little, but Painted Bow's powerful grasp had an air of friendship, and I relaxed.

After I shook hands with the Indians, Grandfather sent Mother off to buy some food. Then he took me into the storeroom and set me down.

"Now, boy," he said, frowning, "out West you got to get yourself dressed proper. Them wool things of yours just itch. They's okay for Laramie, but you got to get some good tough things for the trail. Trader's got to look like half an Indian, otherwise the tribes figure he's a government man."

"Is it a good life being a trader?" I asked.

"Best life around for a white man these days. Mountain

men mostly scout for the Army or for the wagon trains. The trappers been gone for a while."

"What about being a soldier?" I asked. "Isn't it good for a man to be a soldier?"

"Depends. Nowadays most of these soldiers ain't no good at all. When I first came out here, soldiers weren't half bad." Grandfather frowned.

"Now all they want to do is shoot Indians and build forts and railroads. They's killing the West," he said.

"Then I guess I'd better try being a trader," I said.

"Good boy," he said, patting me on the shoulder so hard I almost fell out of the chair. "Now strip."

"What?" I asked.

"Get outa them clothes, boy. Got to get you into some good boots and buckskin."

"I've got shoes," I said.

"Them Philadelphia shoes'll come apart in the first snow. I got some boots that'll fit you. As for the trousers, we'll have to get them sewn for you."

I peeled off my clothes and stood in my undergarments while he measured me. It wasn't exactly a Philadelphia fitting. Grandfather stretched a tape from heel to waist, then wrapped it around my middle.

"A tailor usually takes a bunch of measurements," I said.

"He does, does he? Maybe you'd be better off to find one of them tailors. Boy, I been making shirts and trousers for nigh on fifty years. They goin' to fit just fine. If they don't, we work you so they do fit."

I laughed at that.

"You sure don't have no meat on you, boy," he said, squeezing my arms. "I never did see a boy so thin. Your ma can cook, can't she?"

"Some," I said. "I never got too much to eat at Grandmother's house. The cook didn't like to cook much, and she never fixed enough for me to have seconds."

"Well, no wonder," he said. "A man can't get meat on his bones without eating his fill. We can take care of that."

He was right, too. That night we ate buffalo steaks and potatoes. I ate until I thought I'd burst. It was good, though, and Mother was happy to see me eat so much.

Later Grandfather laid out some straw in the storeroom for me to sleep on. Then he set out some blankets for me, and I wrapped myself up in them. As I huddled in the cold, I heard footsteps on the floor.

"Johnny?" Mother asked. "Are you all right?"

"Yes," I said.

"Happy to be here?"

"Yes," I said, smiling. "I know I have a lot to learn, but Grandfather seems to like me. I'll make you both proud of me."

"I already am," she told me. "You are a fine young man. Not everyone could have stood a two-thousand-mile journey and a meeting with Trader Jim Howard all in one month."

She left me alone in the room, and I felt a new cold possess me. It was a terribly lonely time for me. For two months I'd slept in the back of a wagon with soldiers or huddled around a campfire with other young people.

There was not a single sound outside, either. I missed the birds and insects chirping away their nighttime chorus. I welcomed sound, any sound. I tossed and turned, trying to force sleep into my body. But nothing worked.

Then I heard something move nearby. I sat up, reaching out with my hands.

"It's all right, boy," Grandfather told me. "I just came by to see how you was. Didn't mean to stir you up."

"You didn't," I told him. "I couldn't sleep. It's too quiet, too lonely."

"Not quite like the trail, is it?" he asked.

"No," I said. "I got used to the soldiers snoring, the animals and the birds stirring about. It's so cold and lonely here."

"I remember a time like that myself," he told me. "I was wintering in the mountains for the first time. I'd fought my way across the mountains a few times with survey parties for the Army. I got to know the Indians and their ways, so I decided to make my life there among them."

"By yourself?" I asked.

"Yes, boy. I didn't mind the solitude until I got my cabin built. Then winter set in, and I was shut away from the world. It was terrible, all cold and lonely."

"Like now," I said. "I feel so empty I'll never get filled up again."

"Ever felt that way before?" he asked.

"Once," I said, frowning. "The night I heard about Father. He was very special, you know. He had a hard side to him, but he was always warm to me. He could tell you a story that would make you feel better no matter how bad you felt."

"A boy needs a man to help him grow up," Grandfather said. "In the tribes, a boy who gets orphaned will be adopted by another warrior."

"The Indians do things strange sometimes, but everything seems to make sense."

"Yes, boy. Your mother grew up around a lot of Indians. That's why you were brought here. You feel lonely 'cause your father is gone, but you just open up and let me be your man. I'm a little old to be taking on a young buck like you, but I know a few things."

"You'll show them to me?"

"All in time," he said. "Do you still feel cold and empty?"

"Not so much," I said.

"Well, let me finish my story. There I was, off in the mountains with snow falling all around me. No one was there to share my thoughts. I thought I could last up there by myself. A lot of trappers did. I decided to find out if I could."

"Did you make it?" I asked.

"I'm here now, ain't I?" he asked, laughing. "But I found out something about myself. I'm no loner. I never again took to the mountains alone during winter. I met a fine woman and took her for my wife. Then your mother came along. A man can take anything when there's someone to share it with.

That's what I wanted to tell you. You got someone to share your worries with."

"Thank you," I told him.

"You goin' to be all right, boy," he said, rubbing my neck.

As he walked away, I knew I would be, too. The cold left, and I was filled with a new hope, a warmth of belonging I'd missed in the past eleven months.

CHAPTER 3

The next morning Mother and Grandfather set to work on my new clothes. By noon I was clad in my new outfit of buckskin trousers, flannel shirt, new leather boots, and hat. To round out my outfit Grandfather handed me a soft deerskin jacket. I looked at myself in a small mirror of Mother's, admiring my new appearance.

"Well, boy, what do you think?" Grandfather asked.

"I look like Daniel Boone," I said, smiling.

"Boone?" Grandfather asked. "More like Jim Bridger if you ask me."

Now that I had western clothes, Grandfather began showing me around Fort Laramie. At first he just pointed out the headquarters, barracks, supply buildings, stables, and the like. Then he showed me some of the officers' houses. Finally he introduced me to the line of little shops and houses which, like our own, were owned and operated by civilians.

I got acquainted with most of the soldiers who had stayed at the fort. Sergeant O'Brien and most of the other veterans had ridden east to join the forces defending the Union from the attacks of the rebels.

The war itself didn't matter to me anymore. It was all happening in another world. I guess I felt like the Indians did, that what happened across the great waters belonged to that other world.

I'd met some of the Indians. There were many like Painted Bow who came to the store to trade hides or beadwork for ammunition. It was possible for most of the Indians to get some ammunition from the Army, but most of the warriors preferred to deal with Grandfather. He was honest, and he didn't ask questions.

I assumed the ammunition was being used for hunting, but I soon realized even a great hunter like Painted Bow could not shoot up so many bullets. It was never talked of, but Grandfather and the Indians shared the knowledge that sooner or later there would once again be war with the whites.

Mother refused to allow me to walk beyond the grounds of the fort to visit the soldiers' encampment or the Indian villages. I had little time for it anyway. Grandfather worked me long and hard at the store. I swept floors, packed hides for shipping, restocked shelves, and helped with figures.

"You got a head for figures, boy," he'd tell me. "You do them numbers."

I accepted the compliment with a smile, but I'd rather he told me I was growing taller or stronger or that I was proving to be a help to him. Those were the things he always said to the young Indians.

As the winter snows piled deeper and deeper around the little store and house, our business declined. The Indians didn't hunt as much in the winter, relying on stores of pemmican and flour for food.

Grandfather sold mainly to the soldiers and their wives now. They bought every item imaginable. Most of the new men came to the store for warm coats. The winter was harsh and cold, and Grandfather had been right about my eastern clothes. The deerskin kept out the dampness and chills of winter.

I turned eleven that winter. Mother planned a special dinner for me, and Grandfather arranged for several boys from the post to attend. It wasn't really a party, but I did get a chance to meet some people my own age.

The other boys were bigger, healthier than I was. They looked as if they belonged in the West. I still had too much of the East in me. But they seemed to welcome me into their midst.

Two of the boys, Bill Johnson and Louis Franklin, were sons of army officers. They'd heard of my father's death, and they made me feel welcome. The others were sons of civilians. They were less friendly, and I didn't feel I belonged with them at all.

When the boys had all returned to their homes, Mother took me off to the kitchen and showed me her gift. It was a beautiful new deerskin shirt, soft and wonderfully tooled.

"It's too big for you now, Johnny," she told me. "I made it for you to grow into. I know you will very soon. You seem to be bigger and stronger every day."

I smiled at her, and she gave me a great hug.

"Thank you, Mother," I said. "I will get bigger very soon, too. That way I'll be more help to you and Grandfather."

Grandfather's gift was very different. It was a new hunting rifle, a fine gun that was hard to come by in Laramie. I knew that although Grandfather didn't say so his gift was his way of telling me he was pleased with me.

"Thank you, Grandfather," I told him. "I'll practice until I can shoot it as good as you. I know that will take some time, but I'm a fast learner."

"Know that," he said. "Now that you're most of a man, boy, I think you might call me by my name, Trader Jim. That's what most everybody calls me, and I think you ought to, too."

"You sure?" I asked. "It doesn't seem like that's quite respectful."

"It's what I want you to call me, boy," he told me. "If it grieves you to call me that, though . . ."

"No, sir," I said. "If it's what you want, it's what I want."

Grandfather had one other surprise for me. One day while I was working hard at restocking the shelves, he pulled me off to one side.

"Boy, get your coat and come with me," he said.

I did, wondering what he had in mind. It was snowing outside, and clouds of the white fluff were blowing across the narrow avenues of the fort.

"You go to school back East?" he asked me.

"Yes, sir," I said. "Before Father went to war, I went to the post schools. Most of the time, some officer's wife did the teaching. In York, Mother took me to the school in town sometimes. The teacher there would tell me what to read and study, and I'd do most of it at home. I learned to do figures. I can read pretty good, too, and I have good handwriting."

"You miss the schooling?" he asked me as we plowed our way through the heavy snowdrifts.

"Some," I said. "But Mother has some books, and she works me through them. There are other things to learn besides figures and letters. You'll teach me those things."

"But schooling's still important," he said. "Would you like to go to school here?"

"I wouldn't be able to help out in the store as much," I said. "That's more important."

"If you went to the post school run by old Mrs. Phillips, you wouldn't be able to do anything. But there's another school in Laramie. It's run by a Quaker woman, Mrs. Putnam. She takes in anyone, and she teaches 'em what she can when she can."

When we arrived at the little Quaker mission near the gate, we walked inside. In a small room just inside the door Mrs. Putnam sat down at a table surrounded by boys and girls. There were a few children from the civilian population of the fort, but most were young Indian boys.

"Mrs. Putnam," my grandfather said. "This is my grandson, John Whitlock. He'd like to join your class."

"Welcome, John," she said. "Bring thyself in and meet thy classmates."

I walked with her over to the table, watching the suspicious eyes of the others follow me.

"Meet thy classmates, John," she said. "This is Shirley Ames, Agnes Ann Gurney and Sarah Bryant," she said, showing me the three smiling girls. "Here are the young men," she told me. "Walter Gurney, Jimmy Flynn, Red Fox, Antelope Foot, Bear Tooth, and Little Hawk."

"I'm honored to meet you," I said, watching the eyes of the Indian boys in particular.

"Hello," one of the white boys said. "You're Trader Jim Howard's grandson? I heard about you."

I realized that boy's name was Jimmy something. Walter Gurney had been to my birthday dinner.

Mrs. Putnam didn't make any big thing out of me being there. She just handed me a book and set me to work.

"Have thee ever read, John?" she asked.

"Yes, ma'am," I said. "I do figures, too."

"Thee shall read of the founding of thy country, John. Pages seventy to eighty-four."

I set to work reading. It was a difficult story, full of strange names and dates. But I worked hard at it. I realized Mother's books had not taught me as much as I'd thought. Still, I was better at figures than any of the others, and I'd get better at the reading.

That afternoon I told Mother all about the school.

"If you wished to go to school, you should have told me," she said. "Colonel Henderson would have welcomed you at the post school. You would have had your friends Bill and Louis there, too."

"But Mrs. Putnam has Indians at her school. She's better at teaching than those ladies at the post schools in the East. She knows so many things, too."

"Indians!" Mother screamed. "The very idea."

"But you grew up around Indians," I objected.

"I never went to school with them. There are things you need to learn that Indians will never need."

"I'll have time for those things later," I said. "Just think of how much I can learn from the Indians."

"You can learn all that from your grandfather."

After dinner, Mother and Grandfather argued long and loud about the school. When they finished, Grandfather came in to see me.

"Boy, how was your day at Mrs. Putnam's school?" he asked me.

"Fine," I said.

"Do you mind going to school with Indians?" he asked.

"No, sir," I said.

"Would you rather go to the post school?"

"No, Grandfather," I said. "I wouldn't be able to help around the store much then."

"I thought you were going to call me Trader Jim," he said. "You think you can manage that?"

"Yes, sir," I said. "If you can call me Johnny instead of 'Boy.'"

A smile spread across my grandfather's face. Then he took me in his big hands and lifted me into the air.

"You'll make a fine man, Johnny," he said. "You got courage and understanding. Old Trader Jim'll teach you the ways of the mountains soon, and you'll be a regular trader yourself."

"I hope so," I said.

CHAPTER 4

The winter of 1862 passed, and spring brought sunshine and warmth. New life came to the prairies and the mountains. Animals and birds were everywhere.

Fewer soldiers roamed the fort now. The officers were mostly wounded veterans of the war in the East, and only raw recruits filled the ranks of the enlisted men.

My only two real friends on the post disappeared in March. Bill and Louis accompanied their fathers to Missouri. The men were promoted and sent South to join the campaign against the rebels in Tennessee.

By this time I was the prize pupil of Mrs. Putnam's little school. I was reading and writing everything, and I could do my figures blindfolded.

One day as I was sitting on the small porch of the store doing my figures in the crisp spring afternoon, I felt someone close to me. Looking up, I spotted Antelope Foot, one of the boys from Mrs. Putnam's school. He'd never spoken to me at the school, and I was surprised to see him at the store where he'd never been, either.

"Hello," I said to him. "Did you need something from the store?"

He looked away from me a minute. Then I noticed he had a tablet and a pencil in his hand. I'd never seen any of the Indians take tablets with them. Of all the assembled tribes that visited Fort Laramie, only a handful of Indian boys ever attended the small school. Very few of them spoke English.

"Mrs. Putnam say you do figures good," Antelope Foot said at last.

"I have to," I said. "I help my grandfather with the records in the store. When people need you, you have to do many things."

"This is so," he spoke with his deep, somber voice. His eyes flashed with intensity, and he sat down beside me. He couldn't have been much older than I was, but he was much taller and stronger.

"Do you help your father?" I asked.

"I go on hunt. I kill much game. I be Sioux warrior like my father."

I watched the pride shine across his face as he spoke of his father. I thought back to the times when I had said the same things about my father. He'd only been gone for a year and a half, and I did have Trader Jim Howard for a grandfather. Still, I missed my father.

"You have sadness," the Indian boy said. "Is something I say?"

"No," I said. "I was just thinking about my own father."

"He great warrior?"

"Yes," I said, frowning. "He was killed in the great war in the East. He led a charge against the enemy, and they shot him."

"Is great sadness to lose father. My mother die when I very small. Only know seven summers with her. Great hole inside me."

"Yes," I said, looking at him. "But my grandfather says death is part of life, just like birth. You have to go on."

"Trader is wise man," Antelope Foot said. "My father know him from time of great trappers. He tell of Trader and first wagons crossing buffalo valleys."

"Who is your father?" I asked.

"He called Painted Bow."

"I know of him," I said. "He is a great man."

"He tell of you. That why I come to you. I never can go to other white boy. They not understand. They not like Antelope Foot. They say bad things to me when I not in school."

"What can I do?" I asked. "I'm not very good at things."

"Father say I must learn figures. I take Painted Bow's place in council one day. Important Sioux know words of white man on treaty. We promised much food, many bullet. Some of these things never come. White man make us make mark for things he say we get. We not know if he cheat us."

"You want me to help you with your figures?" I asked.

"You do this, I bring you buffalo hides."

"I'll help," I said, "but not for buffalo hides. I'll show you your figures, and you can show me how to work the hides. My grandfather shows me how to tan the hides, but not how to use dyes and make designs like the Indians do."

"Very simple thing to do," he said, smiling. "Sioux learn this as boy. Is thing squaw does. I teach you."

It turned out to be what Trader Jim called a bargain fairly struck. I learned from Antelope Foot how to take a small piece of deerskin and turn it into a work of art. He also taught me much about the Sioux way of life.

For my part, I taught him the use of figures. He'd always understood that numbers of lodges or buffalo were important, but now he saw how numbers could mean the difference between enough to eat and hunger, between bullets to shoot and being unarmed.

Trader Jim also taught me much. From him and Antelope Foot I learned to notice the difference between the Sioux and Cheyenne, the Arapaho and Shoshoni, the Crow and Kiowa and Pawnee.

I learned the use of the knife as well as the rifle. For the first time, I felt I was a man of the West. I could build a fire, cook my dinner, construct a shelter, defend myself against an enemy.

Trader Jim was proud of me, too. He watched me grow solid. I would never be husky like Walter Gurney or the other boys who lived on the post, but my shoulders were firm, muscular, and there was less of the softness found in a boy and more of the hardness demanded of a man.

Mother was less happy with the new me. I was not yet twelve, and she loved the softness I had brought with me from the East. She tried to encourage my interest in books, in music. But I was captured by the West, and my heart longed for the day when Trader Jim would take me with him on his trips to the Cheyenne and Arapaho villages to the south.

One day when Painted Bow, Many Blankets, and two other Sioux warriors came into the store with many buffalo hides, Trader Jim motioned for me to count the hides. I took my tablet and counted them. There were twenty-six, and I counted twice to make sure I had the right total.

"You should have brought Antelope Foot to check the total," I said to the Indians. "He's very good at figures now."

"We know of this," Many Blankets said. "But a man knows the hearts of his friends. If a friend's heart is not to be trusted, then the sun does not shine in the sky."

"Johnny," Trader Jim said, "what Many Blankets is saying is that when you trade with a man you trust, he won't cheat you. When Painted Bow brings in a buffalo hide, I know it is a good hide. It's been brushed and soaked. I pay him a good price. He knows I won't cheat him because we've hunted together. We've traded lives too many times."

"Traded lives?" I asked.

"Painted Bow has saved mine, and I've saved his. After this happens once, then both lives are owed, and a bond is formed," Trader Jim explained.

"Is it always like that?" I asked.

"It should be," my grandfather told me. "Sometimes the men are not strong, though. But if a man saves my life, it is his right to take it whenever he wishes."

"Not according to law," I said.

"There are laws, and there are laws," Trader Jim said. "The law which governs Painted Bow and me is a higher law than the one some fat senator makes in Washington. It is the law of the mountain, the law of the Sioux and the Cheyenne. It is the law of men, of survival."

"Yes, sir," I said.

That evening Painted Bow and Many Blankets brought their families to the fort for a feast. Trader Jim had a steer barbecued, and we all ate to our heart's content. After eating, everyone moved into a circle. The Indians danced for us, their bright costumes and somber music telling much about their way of life.

Then the contests began. Trader Jim and Painted Bow took turns throwing knives into a tall wooden post. I realized for the first time that my grandfather was still a mighty man. He hurled the knife perhaps forty feet dead into the center of the post. After half an hour had passed, though, they both tired of the sport, and others took their turn.

When Trader Jim had proved he was the finest shot with a rifle, he turned and searched the crowd with his eyes.

"Those games should be for boys," my grandfather bellowed out. "Where's Johnny?"

"Here," I said.

"Son, get in there and test yourself. Pick an opponent."

I glanced along the line of Indian boys. Antelope Foot had fire in his eyes. There were others who would have made a fairer match for me, but I pointed to Antelope Foot.

Painted Bow smiled at me, then nodded his head.

"It is well," Painted Bow said.

"The small trader has a great heart," Many Blankets said. "But he may find that courage is not enough to win."

I smiled at his words. He was likely right. Trader Jim set us across from each other and explained the rules. The first man to hold his opponent's back to the ground would be the winner.

I moaned as I looked at Antelope Foot. He was bigger, stronger, quicker. I ignored all that, though, and went after him. Antelope Foot gave me a quick poke with his shoulder, but I dropped to one knee and grabbed his legs. He shook hard, trying to dislodge me, but I gritted my teeth and hung on.

That was all I could do, though. Try as I could, I couldn't bring him to the ground. I finally tried to grab his waist, but he squirmed away. Then he leaped on my back and forced me to my knees.

His size began to tell, but I wasn't ready to lose yet. I'd never lost at anything, and I hated the idea of letting my grandfather down. But Antelope Foot was powerful, and he threw me to the ground. I tried to get up, but he had me pinned before I knew it. The Indians howled, and Antelope Foot stood up, beaming with pride.

I stumbled to my feet, looking at my toes. Then I walked away from the others and found a lonely spot to sit down.

Mother walked over and put her delicate arm on my shoulder.

"Johnny, you did your best," she said. "You have to understand that these Indian boys are trained to fight from the day they're born. You never had a chance."

"I had a chance," I said. "I wasn't strong enough. But I'll win next time."

"It isn't important, Johnny," she said. "It's just one of those things. Boys have a wrestling contest. One of them has to lose."

"Don't you see?" I asked her. "I let Trader Jim down. He expected me to win. I just proved I'm weak."

"Don't talk like a fool, Johnny," Trader Jim said, picking me up in his powerful arms. "You just proved you had the heart to try. I wouldn't expect you to wrestle a grizzly bear, neither. You did your best. You gave old Antelope Foot a scare. He couldn't shake you."

"But I lost."

"You'll have other chances. They have a race in a little while. I see you run all over that parade ground. You see if you can't beat 'em running."

"You think I can?" I asked him.

"Sure, son," he said, smiling at me. "If you can beat Antelope Foot. He runs like a deer, you know."

Like an antelope, I thought to myself. But I walked up and took my place with the others just the same.

The race was to be a short one, just down to the flagpole and back. It was maybe two hundred yards.

I lined up alongside Antelope Foot and gave him a look of

determination. He smiled back, showing with his eyes that he intended to win again. Then the gun sounded, and we were off.

Antelope Foot got off to a lead, but I closed it quickly. He ran with a long loping stride. My feet stepped off the yards in shorter, choppier chunks, but I gained on him. Making the turn around the flagpole, I stepped out into the lead.

On the return dash I could feel his body close behind mine. He ran hard, but I ran as if my life depended on winning that race. I could see the shine in Trader Jim's eyes as he waited for us, and I didn't intend to dim it.

I raced the last twenty yards like a flash of lightning, leaving the others behind. Antelope Foot crossed a few seconds after me, and the rest of the runners stumbled in later.

The Indians shouted and whooped, and Trader Jim lifted me off the ground and into the air.

"Did you ever see a run like that?" he boomed out. "Finest run I ever saw."

As he put me down, Antelope Foot fell against me, smiling in an admiring way.

"You run like wind," he said. "I very fast. I get name from chasing antelope as boy. You have great heart, Johnny Trader."

He'd never called me by my name, and I laughed when he said that.

"My name isn't Trader," I said. "It's Whitlock."

"I not know this," he said. "We find good name for you soon. Whit—lock. No good name for great warrior. We find you one."

That night I slept well. I'd earned Trader Jim's praise, and I'd proven myself—to him, to the Sioux and to myself.

CHAPTER 5

As spring unfolded its special beauty to the Platte Valley, I put aside my school lessons and accepted a new role in the world. Since my race with Antelope Foot, Trader Jim had accepted me as a true grandson, fit to be included in his world of traders and Indians.

I began to learn the ways of my grandfather's business as I stood beside him day after day. I came to imitate the quiet manner in which he greeted the Sioux warriors who rode in to trade hides for goods. I learned a special smile that could be given to the wives of army officers who came to buy piece goods or cooking pots. I became such a fixture at the store that no one came inside without greeting me or inquiring where I was.

One morning when the snows had finally left the plains, Trader Jim took me by the hand and led me into the supply room.

"Johnny, it's time you got some education," he told me. "Now that the snows have left the valleys, we will go into the business of trading, trading the way it used to be."

"I don't understand," I said. "What are we going to do?"

"Well, son, first of all, you're goin' to get some education. If you're goin' to live out here and become a trader, you got to know the tribes, got to learn to treat with them."

"How do I do that?" I asked.

"You walk these next three days with your eyes and ears open. You notice every word, every movement, every laugh and every smile. You see the Sioux at the fort. Before long you'll be able to tell the Oglala from the Brule and Hunkpapa. But you've seen little of the other tribes."

"I saw some Kiowa down at Fort Hays," I said.

"Could you spot the difference between an Oglala Sioux and a Kiowa on horseback from three hundred yards away?"

"No," I said, looking at my feet.

"You will," Trader Jim said, patting me on the shoulder. "We go tomorrow to the villages of the Cheyenne and the Arapaho. You will come to know them as well as you know your own nose."

"What will we do there?" I asked.

"Son, we do what we always do, trade. We'll load up a wagon with shot and powder and trade goods. Then we'll ride out to the villages. All this time you will be at my side. You will smile at everyone with your officer's lady smile, all the while listening and learning."

"I will listen, and I'll learn, too," I told him.

Before daybreak, Trader Jim shook me awake. I yawned away my tiredness, then scrambled to my feet.

"Let's step lively, son," he told me. "Get into your pants and let's go."

"What time is it, Trader Jim?" I asked, moaning. "I feel like I just went to bed."

"Just about the truth," he said. "Be three hours before the sun's up."

"Why so early?" I asked, stepping into my trousers and pulling them up over my bare legs. "It's still cold."

"Will be most of the time. You'll get used to the bite of the cold. Now give me a hand with the goods."

"Yes, sir," I told him.

It took us more than an hour to stuff a wagon with all the powder, bullets, and knives my grandfather thought would be needed. Then we began loading bright beads, polished glass, and the other trinkets the Indians were fond of.

"Isn't this cheating the Indians?" I asked Trader Jim.

"No, son," he said, laughing. "Squaws like shiny things. A

good trader always carries the goods others want. It's the first law of good trading."

"I guess I should quit asking stupid questions," I said. "When I'm older, I'll know better."

"Son, that's the way a man learns," he told me. "Never sit around when you don't know something. Ask me. A man only grows when he's learning."

"Yes, sir," I said, giving him a bright smile. "I am growing some, aren't I?"

"Sure are, Johnny," he said, smiling back at me. "Now let's get the rest of these goods loaded. We don't get out pretty soon, daylight's going to catch us still unhitched."

I hurried to load the wagon with the rest of the goods while Trader Jim brought the horses out from the stable. Once they were hitched to the wagon, we set out from the fort.

I smiled when we passed the sentries. They came to attention and saluted sharply. I remembered the way the sentries always saluted me when I went to visit my father at the army posts. I returned the salute with my small hand the same as I had before, watching the soldiers laugh at me. Then we rolled out onto the plains of southern Wyoming.

I once heard the prairie compared to a sea. In many ways, that was true. Between the Laramie Mountains and the fort only the North Platte split an ocean of yellow grasses.

We traveled for hours without seeing anything but small shrubs and grasses covering the coulees that bordered the small creek alongside which we traveled.

"Are the villages a long ways off?" I asked Trader Jim.

"The village of the Arapaho is some ways off," he told me. "We go there first. Then we seek out the Cheyennes."

It was well past noon when we finally rode within sight of the Arapaho camp. Three men rode out on horseback to greet us, waving their rifles wildly in the air.

"Do they know we're friendly?" I asked my grandfather.

"They've seen me come many times," he told me. "But the wise thing to do when coming into an Indian camp is to ride forward to meet them, raising your hand above you so they can see you're not preparing to shoot."

"Is it safe then?" I asked.

"Most of the time. Sometimes there may be some young buck in the tribe who's wanting a white man's scalp to hang on his lodge pole. Maybe some kid from the tribe is down with a white man's sickness. Then they get downright hostile."

"What do you do when that happens? How do you know they aren't friendly?"

"Paint's part of it. If they got paint on their faces, paint on their horses, you'd best make a break for it."

"I couldn't outrun an Indian very long," I said.

"Then, son, you do what the Cheyennes do. Sing your death chant. They'll kill you for sure."

"Is it always like that? Is it dangerous to ride here?"

"Johnny, everything that's worth doing in this life has dangers that go with it. For white men I don't think it's any worse than for the Indian. With all the wagon trains and survey parties cutting across their lands, they can be gunned down without a second thought. Most white men don't feel the slightest regret at gunning down an Indian, even if they're Crow or Arikara, very peaceful tribes. If they're Sioux or Cheyenne, the Army just thinks that's a couple less bucks they'll have to fight when the war back East is over."

"You think there'll be a war out here when the war against the South is over?"

"Everyone out here does," Trader Jim said.

"Then why don't the Indians attack now?" I asked. "We don't have enough soldiers to defeat them."

"It's not their way," he told me. "You don't understand the Indians yet. When you do, then you'll know why. That's going to take some time. You've got lots of that, though."

I couldn't tell him of the urgency I felt to be big and strong and grown up. I couldn't tell him I felt I was a man trapped in the body of a boy. He wouldn't have understood the need I felt to be a man, and besides that, he was busy with the Indians.

The lead warrior rode straight for our wagon, crying out some greeting in the language of his tribe. Trader Jim answered him, jumping down from the wagon and running to him. I took the discarded reins and drew the horses to a halt. It was all I could do to stop them.

"Son, come down here," Trader Jim shouted to me.

I tied the reins to the brake and slid down the side of the wagon to the ground.

"You did a good job with the wagon, son," he told me. "Now meet your first Arapaho warrior, Eagle Claw."

I looked up at the young warrior on horseback. He was naked except for a breechclout of red cloth and a necklace of animal teeth.

"What do I say?" I asked Trader Jim.

"Raise your right hand in friendship and tell him you are honored to know him," Trader Jim told me in a soft voice. "He doesn't speak English well, but he'll understand what you say."

I turned to face the Indian, trying to smile at the grim face and fierce body of the man. Then I raised my hand, swallowing deeply.

"I am Johnny Whitlock," I said. "I am honored to meet the great warrior of the Arapaho, Eagle Claw."

"I honored," he answered me, reaching out to clasp my arm with his powerful hand. Then, to my surprise, he pulled me up behind him on his horse.

As my grandfather returned to the wagon and directed it into the Arapaho village, I struggled to hang on to the sweat-streaked back of the Arapaho warrior. He finally set me down, nervous and scared, at the foot of a brightly painted tepee.

"You all right?" Trader Jim asked me. "You look a might shaky."

"A might," I said, shivering. "It's not that it was all that scary. It's just that he surprised me."

"A might?" Trader Jim asked me.

"More than a might," I said, breaking into a bright smile. "A lot more," I added, laughing.

Trader Jim led me to the back of the wagon where he directed me to take various items out. I placed them in front and to each side of where my grandfather was sitting. The polished stones and beads were directly in front of him. The other things were spread out all around him so that the Indians could see them clearly and Trader Jim could reach them all.

"Come over here, Johnny," he called to me at last. "Sit down right beside me. Try to smile as much as you can. The Arapaho like smiling boys. But whatever you do, don't accept anything without looking at me. They will respect you for honoring my opinions, and I will point to something if there's a need to return the gift in kind."

"Yes, sir," I said, folding my legs underneath me the way he had. "Is there anything else?"

"Just not to talk unless they speak directly to you, and in English. Otherwise, turn to me. Language barriers can be downright dangerous. Later you will learn to speak the tongues of the plains tribes. For now, just remember most of these men are warriors. They live by a code of honor, and very few of them have not killed."

"Yes, sir," I told him.

It didn't take long for the Arapaho to arrive. Most of them knew my grandfather from past times. Several of the men spoke to me in passing, but I didn't understand a word of their language. I turned to my grandfather, but he shook his head. I just opened my mouth wide and grinned my best. They smiled in reply.

One of the Indian women came by after a few minutes and gently touched my hair. There was a tenderness to her touch, and I smiled at her, too. She handed me a small pouch made of some soft skin, and I tapped Trader Jim on the shoulder.

"Should I take it?" I asked him.

"Yes, son," he told me. "It's a great honor. Give her one of the polished stones. She'll like that."

"Yes, sir," I said.

I reached down and took one of the stones. Then I handed

it to her. The look that lit her eyes told me she was pleased by this great treasure I had presented her with.

I watched Trader Jim the rest of the afternoon. He talked to me as he exchanged powder or shot or trade goods with the Indians for skins or beadwork. I tried to figure out what he was really doing, but it didn't get through to me. He traded with each man fairly. I figured for a trader to stay in business he had to make a little profit on every deal.

"No, son," my grandfather told me. "Never trade without honor. Never trade above or below the value of something. If you trade below your own value, you teach a man to steal. If you trade above your own value, the other trader will carry a grudge for you the rest of his days."

"But how do you profit?"

"By selling the best of each world to the other. I sell to the Indian what is easy to come by for the white man. I sell to the white man what is easy to come by for the Indian. My profit comes as a bridge between the two worlds."

"I see," I said.

"Not yet, but you will. I trade with the Indian. I sell to the whites. Selling involves no exchange, but a trade must be made with honor. To the Cheyenne or Arapaho, the white man is mainly a cheat. Those few of us that are left from the old days are honored even above members of their own tribe because they know we understand. They know they can trust us. They know we are more of their world than the white man's world."

"How is that?" I asked. "How can you be white and still be of the Indian's world?"

"Easy," he said, smiling. "My heart still values honor and courage above silver and gold."

"Courage and honor are valued in the East," I told him. "My father valued both courage and honor."

"Yes, son," Trader Jim said, taking my arm and pulling me close to him. "Johnny, your father was a brave man. He was one of the few idealists left. But for every one of those, there are fifty who would sell their own mother for a thousand dollars. A man only needs a warm place to sleep and enough to eat. And to be left in peace."

"I guess that's not too much to ask," I said, giving him my best smile. "I guess that's all anybody needs."

"It's all the Indian asks," Trader Jim said sadly. "And little enough at that. But I'm afraid the white man has cast his feet upon the buffalo valleys, and he will stamp out all that is in his path."

"I hope not," I said. "I like courage and honor. I think if I have the time, I'll get to be a trader like you."

"Believe you will," he said, slapping my small back with his huge hand.

We pitched our tent beside the wagon that night. As night cast its shadow over the camp of the Arapaho, Trader Jim helped me set out blankets for us. Then he led me over to the great council fire of the chiefs.

"Here you must be silent," he warned me. "The Arapaho do not allow children, even honored guests, to speak at the council. But observe everything you see. This may be the last time you ever visit an Arapaho council fire. Remember it."

"Yes, sir," I said.

The council was a very solemn thing. Only the chiefs spoke. I was fascinated by their colorful costumes. Unlike Eagle Claw, these men wore painted blankets and great feathered war bonnets. Even their leggings bore colorful beadwork.

"They've put on a show for us," Trader Jim told me. "They're decked out in full battle dress. I don't suppose old Iron Chest has had many visitors of late."

"Which one is he?" I asked in a whisper.

At the sound of my voice, eyes flashed in my direction. Trader Jim turned purple, then rose from his place. He spoke some words in the language of the Arapaho, and the chiefs laughed.

"I told them you were only on the prairie for the first time," Trader Jim whispered to me. "Don't say another word."

I bit down hard on my lip and watched the rest in silence. If I'd kept quiet and used my eyes, I would have seen why

Iron Chest was called that. He had a great iron vest which he wore in front of his chest.

The chiefs spoke with my grandfather for hours and hours. They laughed, smiled, frowned. I could tell they spoke of old friends, old times. They also ate an awful mush of some kind which they shared with me. The hardest thing I'd had to do since leaving Laramie was pretend that the mush tasted good.

After dinner there was much dancing and celebrating, and for the first time I saw children. They ran through the fire and danced with the adults. Their faces were bright like mine, but their eyes were fearless.

Somehow without anything being said, I felt I'd learned a great deal. Those children were like Antelope Foot, brave and strong. In their eyes I saw the future warriors of the Arapaho people. I hoped that the greedy foot of the white man might keep itself busy somewhere else long enough for me to learn their ways and enjoy their company.

That night I lay awake, tired but unable to sleep.

"What did you say to the chiefs tonight?" I asked my grandfather.

"We talked of old times," he said.

"Tell me," I said.

"Johnny, we will have many nights on the prairie before we reach the lodges of the Cheyenne. We will have many nights to talk of the old times. Tonight I am tired. Let's sleep."

I lay back on my blanket, but I restlessly tossed back and forth.

"You sleepless?" Trader Jim asked me.

"Yes," I said. "I saw so much, learned so much today."

"Is that all?" he asked me. "This is your first night on the prairie. Do you miss your mother?"

His question surprised me.

"I hadn't thought of that," I said. "All the way out here with the army supply column I spent my time with the soldiers and slept with the soldiers. But she always came to look in on me. Even at Laramie I never really go to sleep until I feel her eyes look in on me. She whispers softly to me sometimes, even though I never answer. I guess it's our own little game. I pretend I'm asleep and don't hear, and she pretends she doesn't know I'm listening."

"Women are like that, son," he said. "I guess she's probably awake right now wondering what you're doing. It takes a special woman to step away and let her son be a man."

"She's always been that way," I said. "It would have been easier for her to stay in the East. She brought me out here so I could have you to help me become a man. I guess I've kind of neglected her lately."

"You do this, son. Find some special thing she'd like. You can trade for it. She'll light up like a campfire when she sees you remembered her while you were out here."

"Yes," I said. "That would be good."

"Now find your peace in sleep," he told me.

"Yes, sir," I said, surrendering to the peaceful darkness that sleep brings to a weary boy.

CHAPTER 6

It took us six days to travel to the encampment of the Cheyenne. It was a long journey over difficult terrain, but it filled Trader Jim with pride to show me the creeks and rivers of the land he knew as home.

Those six days were an education unlike any I was ever to receive again. I learned to walk like a shadow, hunt and fish like a bear, and think like one born to the plains. I saw my first buffalo, caught my first trout, shot my first rabbit. I learned to recognize how the stars point the way, and I came to read the weather.

In those few brief days I left behind all that I had been and began my lifelong struggle to become what I was destined to be. I felt myself grow wiser with the knowledge of the world. And in the quiet moments between assigned tasks I came to know myself as never before.

Running across the prairies after game and dodging the wicked rattlesnakes that abounded there, I grew taller and stronger. And new confidence born of experience filled my heart with warmth.

The best parts of those days were the hours I spent with Trader Jim after the sun went down. We would build a roaring campfire to chase away the bite of the sharp spring wind and spread out our blankets alongside each other. Then I would listen as he related some treasured story of the old days before the forts and the wagons came to the Platte.

My grandfather had been there since the beginning. He had met them all, Bridger, Coulter, Sublette, and Fitzpatrick. He'd hunted the headwaters of the Yellowstone and Missouri.

He'd camped among the Cree and Arikara, the Crow and the Assiniboins, the Blackfeet and the Shoshoni. He was known to the Arapaho, the Cheyenne, and the Sioux. He had ranged in the south through the lands of the Kiowa, Pawnee, and Comanche.

His tales of adventures shared with the men who had opened the West to the white man stirred my heart. I couldn't hear enough of them, and he never seemed to run out. He seemed to have a story for every minute of the day, every day of the year. In his fifty-seven years he had lived life to the fullest, had done all there was to do. Or so I thought.

"No man's ever done all there is to do," he told me one day. "He may think so, but he never knows. Each new dawn holds some new adventure in store for him. I remember when old Jim Bridger and me found a pass across the Rockies."

"You were with Jim Bridger when he found the pass through the Rockies?" I asked. "That was the real breakthrough for the wagon trains. I heard my father say that once."

"Well, Johnny," he said, taking a pinch of chewing tobacco out of the pouch that always dangled from around his neck. "I guess it all started one day way back before you were born."

"Everything way back was before I was born," I said. "When was it?"

"Oh, back in the thirties or forties, I suppose," he said, grinning. "Back then I didn't keep much of a calendar. Anyway, Big Jim and me and old Kit Carson was riding along trying to find a way through the Rockies into California. Now back then California still belonged to the Mexicans."

"My father fought them in a war to get us California," I said.

"Okay, boy," Trader Jim said, frowning. "You goin' to go and let me finish this story or not?"

"Sorry," I said.

"Well, Big Jim and I figured maybe there was a way through them mountains. One day when we was hunting some deer up on a mountainside, what do we come by but a small herd of buffalo."

"Buffalo in the mountains?" I asked.

"Sure enough," he said. "Surprised the devil out of me. I never seen a buffalo off the prairies before. Now Big Jim took a long look at them buffalo. Then he smiled.

"'Trader,' he says to me, 'you know we ain't seen no buff this side of the Rockies since spring. Them ain't Platte buffs.'

"I looked over at him and smiled back. I told him he was thinking maybe them buffalo might just be from the other side of the Rockies. That, son, was exactly where they was from. We followed them buffalo right back through the pass, and the Rockies was open."

"I heard part of that once before," I said. "A sergeant at Laramie told me that it was only just Kit Carson that was with Bridger."

"Well, boy, you can't always believe everything you hear," my grandfather said, laughing to himself.

"From the sergeant or you?" I asked.

"Well, I heard it a lot of different ways. Some say an old Shoshoni chief took Big Jim through the pass. I like the buffalo story better myself."

"Then you weren't really there?" I asked.

"Well, son, I should have been. I was with Big Jim just about everywhere else. I was off trapping some when he found the pass, but if they'd asked me, I could have found them a hundred passes."

"Just as good?" I asked.

"Well, it's a mighty fine pass if you're heading to California."

I laughed at him.

"You have a good head for tales, Trader Jim," I told him. "I believe tomorrow you'll be telling me about how you fought the whole Sioux nation with one hand tied behind your back."

"Thought I already told you that one," he said, smiling.

Our arrival in the Cheyenne village was met with no great stir of excitement. Unlike the Arapaho, the Cheyenne people seemed unimpressed with us. When Trader Jim pulled the brake back on the wagon and tied off the reins, I stood up and prepared to jump to the ground.

"Son, sit back down," Trader Jim told me. "White men don't make the first move into a Cheyenne camp."

I sat down and fashioned my frown after the one my grandfather wore on his stern face. The Cheyenne people walked by the wagon without saying a word. I grew nervous after several of them had passed by, but Trader Jim just bit off a square of chewing tobacco and chewed away on it.

We must have waited for nearly an hour. Then a tall man dressed in buckskin leggings and breechclout approached us.

"This is White Panther, one of their war chiefs," Trader Jim whispered to me.

White Panther walked out in front of the wagon and stopped. Then he raised his right hand and stared at us with eyes full of hatred.

A shudder worked itself through me as I marveled at the bulging muscles in White Panther's arms and shoulders. No part of him gave itself over to weakness or flab.

"I, White Panther, chief of the Cheyenne, greet the great trader from the white man's fort on the Platte," the Indian said in his deep, fearless voice.

"I am honored to be in the presence of the great Cheyenne war chief and his people," Trader Jim told him.

"Why does the trader seek the Cheyenne?" White Panther asked.

"The trader comes to offer goods to the mighty Cheyenne," Trader Jim said.

"The white man comes to give presents to the Cheyenne?" the chief asked, a sly grin coming to his lips. "Does he seek the aid of the Cheyenne to take his presents, or does he come to take from us what is ours? Does he bring guns and bullets?"

"The trader brings as he always has those things which the Cheyenne need. It brings no honor to him to steal from the Cheyenne as others do."

"We are not blind, trader," White Panther said. "We are not some fat Crow who would trade away his brother for shiny stones and beads."

"I have traded with all manner of people, White Panther," Trader Jim told him. "I was walking the lands of the Sioux and Cheyenne when you ran naked through your father's lodge. I cheat no one. I trade only what a man has need of or what he finds pleasure in. I bring no guns for you, but I bring shot and powder which the Cheyenne need to hunt the buffalo and the elk. If White Panther needs new guns to hunt with, he can send warriors to Laramie with buffalo hides. I am no gun runner, and I do not sell spirits."

"You speak mighty words, trader," White Panther said, glaring at us. "But my people have seen many who speak with mighty words. Mighty words do not always prove to be true."

"Your people know me, White Panther," Trader Jim said, growling with impatience. "I have brought my grandson with me to show him the ways of the Cheyenne. I have told him of the grandeur of this nation of proud warriors. I did not know that the Cheyenne now spoke harshly to their guests. We have been on the prairie these six days in search of your camp. We could have traded better with the Sioux or the Kiowa, but it was our wish to greet the Cheyenne in friendship as the brothers we had known in the past."

"Much is written of the white man's past," White Panther spoke. "But the past of the Cheyenne is written in the eyes of our children. In the winter we read hunger there. In the summer we read pain, for the wagons of the white man take many of their fathers from our camp."

"This news weighs on my mind heavily," Trader Jim said. "I see that we bring more pain to the Cheyenne. We will be gone when the sun dies in the west."

Trader Jim released the brake and led the horses to one side.

"Trader!" White Panther yelled. "Do you not bring presents for my brother, Black Kettle?"

"Black Kettle is here?" Trader Jim asked, pulling the reins back to halt the horses. "Does he know I have come?"

"His heart is heavy," White Panther said. "He speaks of nothing."

"This is bad," Trader Jim said. "Black Kettle has always been a friend to me. I have slept in his camp many times. I have hunted the deer with his hunting parties. He is far north of his old hunting grounds."

"The men who come in search of the yellow powder have killed many Cheyenne in the south. Those who remain hunt with us this summer."

"I would not burden my friend Black Kettle, but I would have him know my heart is with him in his trouble. What would he have in the way of presents? Anything that is mine is his."

White Panther's frown softened as he read the sadness in my grandfather's eyes. The chief's eyes brightened, and his mouth broke into a smile.

"I will go and say to Black Kettle that the trader has come. You will wait," White Panther said.

As White Panther turned and walked away, I tapped Trader Jim on the shoulder.

"What's happening?" I asked. "Who is Black Kettle?"

"Don't know for sure what's happening," he told me. "I never thought Black Kettle would let some young buck dog soldier like White Panther speak for the whole camp."

"But who is Black Kettle?" I asked. "And what is a dog soldier?"

"If you are mightily blessed by God, son, you'll one day meet as great a man as Black Kettle, chief of the southern Cheyenne. I never dreamed he'd be this far north. The southern Cheyenne usually hunt buffalo in the south near the Republican River. I heard the people down in Colorado were stirred up against the Cheyenne and Arapaho, but they must be pretty fierce to chase Black Kettle up here."

"And dog soldiers?"

"That's what the Cheyenne call their warriors. They fight like hungry dogs."

"Are they as fierce as the Sioux? Antelope Foot says the Sioux are the fiercest warriors there are."

"As fierce as the Sioux," Trader Jim said grimly. "I hope to God you never have a chance to see just how fierce either of them are."

"They wouldn't attack us, would they?" I asked.

"The tribes are coming into the hands of new chiefs. If Black Kettle has turned his camp over to White Panther, then maybe Red Cloud has turned his camps over, too. Soon the whites will come West in herds, and there will be war again."

We sat in the wagon and waited for White Panther. He returned in a few minutes with a tall Cheyenne warrior dressed in beautiful buckskin shirt and trousers. On his proud head was a war bonnet of eagle feathers. He wore an open blue jacket around his shoulders, one pocket of which bore a bright medal bearing the emblem of the United States of America.

"Black Kettle, old friend and great chief, we are honored to share the light of your presence," Trader Jim said. "My heart is heavy with the news we have of your people."

"It is well to share the sorrow of my people, trader, for it is a sorrow which will overflow the riverbanks and drown you as well," the chief said.

"It is as you say, Black Kettle," my grandfather said, climbing down from the wagon to face him. "The boy is my grandson, Johnny."

"He has brightness in his eyes," Black Kettle said. "There is courage in his face. Has he the strength to see what will come to our land?"

"Johnny, come down here," Trader Jim said, motioning me from the wagon. "He is my daughter's only son, my only grandchild. He is from the other world, but he has the soul of a Cheyenne warrior. He sees in the mountains the hand of the spirit, and he walks the buffalo valleys with a softness that respects the land."

"Come to me, son of the stars," Black Kettle said. "The shine that lights your eyes is of the heavens."

The great chief placed his hands on my shoulders and tested them for firmness. He forced his heavy hands straight down so that I felt he would press me into the ground. But my knees held firm, and a smile crossed the face of the chief.

"Where is your father, son of the stars?" the chief asked.

"He's dead," I said, frowning.

"How did he meet his death?" asked White Panther, turning my head to face him.

"He was a soldier," I said. "A chief. He led his men in battle, but the rebels shot him down."

"He was killed in the war back East," Trader Jim explained.

"My father die in battle," White Panther said. "Is no greater death."

"I'd rather have him here, alive," I sighed.

"This is the voice of the son," Black Kettle said, taking my hand. "Wisdom will come to you, son of the stars."

We traded many knives, barrels of powder, and boxes of cartridges to the Cheyenne that afternoon. I watched as my grandfather accepted less from the Cheyenne than he took from the Arapaho. To the children he gave bright cloth and sugar candy. Where there was hunger, he gave flour and salted bacon. In return, we piled many fine woven blankets and buffalo hides in the back of the wagon.

Before leaving the camp of the Cheyenne, we saw Black Kettle one last time. He took my hand and led me to his lodge. There was a large American flag standing outside, and I stared at it for a moment.

"Given to me by great white father," Black Kettle said with pride. "He say to me that no long knife shoot at Cheyenne who stand beside this flag."

As Black Kettle walked into his lodge, White Panther pulled me aside.

"Cheyenne would trade this cloth of stars to you, white boy, for twenty new rifle. Rifle Cheyenne can trust. Word of white chief is like summer wind. It blow only until winter come," White Panther told me. "But this not your doing. Go with Black Kettle. See what honor there is in his heart."

I walked into the lodge and stepped forward to where Black Kettle was waiting. I felt naked in his presence, powerless, ignorant. I searched for Trader Jim and his wisdom, but they were not there. Whatever would happen, I would have to deal with it on my own.

"Son of the stars," Black Kettle said to me, "I give you something to take you on your journey through life. The first is a knife I have carried myself in battle many times. It is old and worn, but the blade has courage and strength and power. The second is what I see in your eyes. You must trust those eyes and what they see. Trust your heart and your eye, not the words you will hear. Truth comes from the heart, not from the tongue."

"I have little to give in return," I said. "But I have a knife my grandfather gave me. Would you take it in return?"

"A wise man returns a present with a present," Black Kettle said. "To leave another's gift unanswered is to leave one in debt. I take this and send you on your way."

I walked from the lodge, leaving Black Kettle behind me in a solemn stillness. Then I ran to show Trader Jim the knife.

That night at our camp up the creek from the Cheyenne village, I asked Trader Jim why the Cheyenne people seemed so tired.

"They seem like they don't care if they live or die," I said.

"They see their death written in the wind," Trader Jim explained. "They say the white man will come again soon, and the buffalo valleys will be swallowed by his hordes. This is many years away, I hope. I'm not sure I want to live long enough to see it. I guess Black Kettle and some of the others feel that way, too."

"He will fight, though," I said. "At least White Panther will."

"Black Kettle knows what White Panther will learn. There is no victory over the white man. They will try to find peace.

In the end, they will either accept whatever the whites offer them, or our soldiers will ride them down and kill them."

"Which will they do?" I asked.

"Die," he told me. "It's the Cheyenne way. Their death chant says it all. Nothing lives long, only the earth and the sky stay the same."

"Is that what will happen to the Indians? Will they just disappear?"

"How many Indians did you see in Pennsylvania?" he asked me. "They used to live there, too. Most of our states take their names from Indian tribes or Indian words."

"Will it change?" I asked. "Can't we do something?"

"No, son," he said. "We will only live and watch and mourn, just like the Cheyenne."

"And die?" I asked.

"Yes, son," he said, frowning. "And die."

CHAPTER 7

My journey to the camps of the Arapaho and Cheyenne was
like a journey into a different world. When Trader Jim spoke
to the Indians of my being an outsider, he really spoke the
truth. But I was changing, learning, accepting the new life
that had come to me.

As happy as I'd been to greet the prairies for the first time,
I had to admit it was good to return to Laramie. My mother
pretended not to have missed me, but she smiled when I gave
her the deerskin bag I'd brought back for her. That night
when I finally got to bed, she walked in and sat beside me.
Then she stroked my hair.

"I'm glad to be home, Mother," I said to her.

She pulled her hand away and stared at me, surprised.

"I didn't mean to wake you, Johnny," she said.

"I wasn't asleep," I said. "Just thinking. I missed our little
talks and your good night visits."

"You noticed them?" she asked.

"I always did," I said, sitting up. "You knew, too."

"How did you know that?" she asked, her eyes wide with
surprise. "You're not supposed to know everything, Johnny."

"I have to," I told her. "I'm a man, remember?"

"I never wanted to admit it, Johnny," she said. "I've
watched you in the store. I saw the look on your face when
you came back from the plains beside your grandfather. Your
eyes were full of adventure. That was no boy."

"On the outside maybe," I said sadly. "Not on the inside. If
I was man, I wouldn't need you so much."

"I love to hear that, Johnny, but it's only partly true. Out here you'll always want to belong to me, to the East where you came from. But the West has already placed its brand on you. The land out here is the only mother anyone knows. No human mother can compete with the lure of the mountains and the rivers. The Indians know that. So do I. I grew up out here, too."

"What do I do about the part of me that wants to hold on to being a boy?" I asked her.

"Keep it as long as you can, for both of us," she said, shaking a tear from her eye. "But be the man you are. Don't be less than you can be."

"What about you?"

"I'll just fade into the background," she said. "That's the way mothers are. They're always around, but they have to learn they're never a success unless they can let go."

I don't think either one of us understood exactly what we were sharing. But after that night, Mother never again came into my room at night, and I never again slept as warm and secure. From that time on I made my own way in the world, but I always kept a place in my heart for her.

We were back at Fort Laramie off and on the rest of the spring. There was much trading to be done, both with the Sioux and with occasional bands of Cheyenne. We also did much business with the soldiers at the fort, trading fine woven goods and Indian bead- and leatherwork for cash Trader Jim put into Mother's hands.

I never knew what Mother did with the money, for Trader Jim and I never used any of it. Our currency was trade goods, and we kept track of money only on our account books. Mother made out the orders for goods from the East, but those items were always paid for out of the balance owed us for buffalo hides and deerskins.

I went back to school in the mornings, but I learned as much about figures by keeping the store accounts as I ever would have in any school. I went to the school, though, because I needed the companionship of others my age, especially my friend Antelope Foot.

When summer finally came, Trader Jim interrupted my sweeping of the narrow front porch one afternoon.

"Johnny, sit down a minute," he told me.

"Yes, sir," I said.

"You'll be twelve years old in the winter, and all you've ever hunted is rabbits and goats. What would you think about taking a hand in a buffalo hunt?"

"Buffalo?" I asked.

"No Sioux buck worth his supper would spend twelve summers without hunting a buffalo. We got these three young lieutenants in from the East the other day. They been asking me about taking them out. I talked Swift Deer and War Cloud into letting us ride onto the Sioux hunting grounds on a buffalo hunt. If we go, would you want to come along?"

"Of course," I said, my eyes lighting up at the thought. "Do you think I'm big enough to shoot that big buffalo gun of yours?"

"You got the size to do anything you want," he said. "Ain't the size of a man's shoulders matters out here. It's the size of his heart. You got the heart of the mountains, son. But you'd best take that rifle of yours."

"Can you kill a buffalo with a single shot rifle?" I asked him.

"Maybe not with one shot, son, but you hit him twice in the vitals, you got yourself a kill."

We left early the next morning. The lieutenants rode their army horses behind Trader Jim and me. My grandfather rode his trusty old sorrel, and I found myself riding the proud young mustang Painted Bow had traded to us that spring.

When we reached the camp of the Sioux, we met up with War Cloud, Swift Deer, and Painted Bow. With them to my surprise and delight was Antelope Foot.

The men rode in front, leaving perhaps twenty yards of rolling prairie between them and us. It suited Antelope Foot and me to let them ride ahead, for he would not speak in the presence of his elders, and I would not feel comfortable to talk to anyone else.

By midafternoon War Cloud and Swift Deer had left our party to scout ahead. The lieutenants and Painted Bow rode with Trader Jim. Antelope Foot and I still trailed behind.

"Have you seen the herd?" I asked Antelope Foot.

"We have killed many bulls from this herd," he said. "I kill two great bulls not far from here. We soon be there. You will kill buffalo, too, my brother. Have you done this before?"

"No," I said. "I've shot rabbits and goats. Are buffalo different?"

"Not the killing," he said. "But buffalo very hard to kill. Must shoot below shoulder. Shot in middle or tail no good. Buffalo run many moons with arrow or bullet in body. Must kill with good shot."

"Have you ever been afraid to shoot at one?" I asked Antelope Foot, looking into his eyes to find the truth.

"I have no fear, Johnny," he said. "Is not way of Sioux to fear death. You must understand this much," he said, halting his horse. "There is time to die and time to live. Spirits say which this day must be. Sioux understand this. You will come to see this, too."

"But I'm not a Sioux," I said. "I'm afraid."

"There is no fear in the eyes of my friend," he told me. "You will stand and shoot many buffalo. When time come, you will not turn from what must be. You know this as I do."

"I wish I could be as sure," I said.

"If you know own heart as I know it, you would know there is no fear inside you. Johnny, my friend, you would make good Sioux warrior."

"I am honored," I said. "There is no greater praise from a Sioux."

We rode in silence for many minutes. Then we both saw Swift Deer ride over the horizon, waving his rifle in the air.

"Swift Deer find buffalo," Antelope Foot told me. "We go to others."

I spurred the mustang forward. By the time Trader Jim and the others had reached Swift Deer, Antelope Foot and I had arrived, too.

I started to say something, but a glance from Antelope Foot told me to keep silent. War Cloud spoke to Trader Jim, and my grandfather answered. Then Painted Bow, Swift Deer, and War Cloud rode off.

"This is the way we do this," Trader Jim told the lieutenants. "The Sioux will move the herd toward us. We will wait and shoot as the herd runs past."

The lieutenants nodded their heads in agreement, and Trader Jim rode over to us.

"Antelope Foot," my grandfather said, "your father has given his permission for you to stay with Johnny. The two of you can shoot at anything you see once the lieutenants fire, but you have to wait for them to hit or miss. This hunt is for them, not for you. Understand?"

We nodded.

"Then take up stations in the rear," Trader Jim said. "The hides belong to the men who kill the buffalo, but the meat goes to the Sioux. Good luck."

When he had ridden off, I looked at Antelope Foot.

"Why did he say that?" I asked.

"He say to settle questions," Antelope Foot told me. "This to show you how it done. White man not hunt on Sioux land. Say that in treaty. This way white man find courage in hunt, but Sioux not lose buffalo meat."

"Is that all the Sioux get?" I asked.

"Soldiers give War Cloud five new rifle for hunt."

"They'd better hit something then," I said, laughing.

Before either of us could say anything else, we felt the ground tremble with the thunder of buffalo hoofs. I kept one eye on the great herd, the other on the lieutenants.

The lieutenants fired together, and one bull shuddered. There were more shots, but I was too busy to notice their effects. I swung my rifle around and picked out a great bull lumbering toward me.

I aimed right below the bull's right shoulder, but I waited for it to near me. Antelope Foot raced out to cut off the herd, firing as he rode. I stood my ground as he had said, firing only when the bull was upon me. Then I spurred the mustang away, watching the bull go down not fifteen yards from where I stood.

Four bulls were killed that day; Antelope Foot and I killed three of them. The lieutenants killed the other one. Trader Jim and the others had not hunted.

Antelope Foot helped me strip the monsters of their hides, and we left the bloody carcasses for the others to carry to the Sioux camp. The lieutenants took their hide, and I carried mine.

"You have taken your first buffalo, my brother," Antelope Foot said to me as we prepared to part company. "This makes you a warrior, a true brother to me. We will hunt many times, Johnny. When the cold winds come, we will hunt the bighorn sheep in the mountains. Many deer will fall to our rifles."

"Yes," I said, smiling. "We will share great adventures."

As Trader Jim and I led the soldiers back to the fort, he wore a smile of approval on his face.

"You did yourself proud," my grandfather told me, reaching out his hand to slap my shoulder. "That was no small thing to kill such a big bull. It's not an easy kill to take such a beast that way. You miss, you're buffalo dust."

"I was afraid," I said to him, hanging my head. "But Antelope Foot was there, and he told me I wouldn't back away. I couldn't show fear with him there."

"Son, it's not fear you had in your heart then. It takes more courage to face doubt when you need to prove yourself than to go out and charge some fool enemy that's got to kill you. Real courage is doing what you have to when you have to."

"Like my father," I said.

"Like him," Trader Jim said. "And like you, son."

I received much praise at the fort for my bravery. I told the story of my adventure many times those next few days. With Antelope Foot around from time to time to echo my story, I was a hero to the other boys and a wonder to the young soldiers at the fort.

I turned the buffalo hide over to my mother. She turned it

into a great coat for me, one that would keep the winter chill from my bones. "Now you have a coat for a man," she said to me. "You can go into the Powder River Valley this winter to hunt deer with Antelope Foot, and I won't have to worry about your health."

"You'll always worry," I told her. "And I'll always miss you when I'm away."

"Your father would have been proud of you, Johnny," she said, choking with a sob she'd never give way to in front of me. "He would have wanted to take your hand and tell you himself."

"I wish he was here," I said sadly. "Not just for me. If Father was still alive, life would be easier on you."

"No, Johnny," she said. "It wouldn't be too different. I'd still have the house to tend to, my sewing and knitting to do. I might be on some other army post, but I'd be an army wife. It's the life I was born to live."

"We all have our lives to live," I said. "What was I born to be?"

"You'll find that out for yourself," she said. "In a few more years your life will come to you."

"What would you want me to be?" I asked. "A trader like Trader Jim? An army officer like Father? An army scout, a gold miner?"

"None of those," she said. "But this is not the time to speak of it. Later."

There was a look of mystery in her eye, and I wondered what she meant. But those summer days were too full of adventure for me to dwell on Mother's strange mood.

CHAPTER 8

The summer came and went in the midst of buffalo hunts and fishing trips. The Platte and the creeks to the south provided many fine afternoons of swimming and fishing, and I came to know them as well as Trader Jim did.

Autumn is striking on the plains. Everything blazes in a golden tint, and the cold nights are forgotten in the midst of the warm afternoons.

In September I spent every afternoon with Antelope Foot, helping him with his figures the way he'd helped me learn the rivers and creeks that summer. He was quick of mind, and he came to be as agile with numbers as he was on the painted pony he rode across the prairie.

Then one day Antelope Foot came no more. At first I just figured the Sioux had sent him with a hunting party to the Powder River Valley. But Antelope Foot had promised to take me along when it came time to go north, and I was confused.

When he had been gone for three days, I saddled my horse and rode out to the Sioux camp on the Platte. The Sioux had grown accustomed to seeing me in the company of Antelope Foot or my grandfather, but I never before rode into the camp alone.

I felt a tremor of uncertainty inside me, for the Sioux stared at me with hostility. There was no friendship in the eyes of the people, and I felt cold. Part of me wanted to turn and ride away, but I missed my friend, and I worried that something was wrong.

I tied the mustang to a small bush and walked into the camp. My eyes searched everywhere for Antelope Foot, but he was not to be found. Then a young warrior named Snake Nose walked over and stood in my way.

"Why do you come here, white boy?" he asked. "You are not welcome in the camp of the Sioux."

"I have always been welcome here in the past," I said. "I come in search of my friend, Antelope Foot."

"He does not search for you. He knows where you are. If he wishes to find you, he will," Snake Nose told me.

"But he might need me. We help each other," I explained.

"Leave this place, white boy," the Indian told me. "He needs you no more."

"I must see him," I said, stepping forward.

"Do you not have eyes, white boy?" Snake Nose asked me in anger. "Do you not read the signs of mourning in this camp? Can you not see no white man is welcome here? This is a time for the Sioux to mourn. No white man will be welcome here for many moons."

"What has happened?" I asked. "I have to know."

"Know only this," Snake Nose said, hatred flashing in his eyes. "If you do not turn and ride away, there will be mourning in the lodge of the trader this night, for your scalp will rest on my lodge pole."

I stepped back and looked him straight in the eye.

"If you would kill me, then do it," I said. "If this is my day to die, then it must be."

Snake Nose looked at me with surprise in his eyes.

"Antelope Foot taught me that," I said. "We have shared too many things for me to walk away without seeing him."

"He sees no man," Snake Nose said, frowning. "Go back to fort."

"I will see this man," spoke the voice of my friend, Antelope Foot, from behind us. "He comes in peace, Snake Nose. He has no understanding of the thing that has happened. I will talk to him."

Snake Nose moved aside, and I walked to Antelope Foot. My friend was much changed. His eyes were full of sadness, and he pulled a thin blanket around his shoulders.

"What's wrong?" I asked him. "Are you sick?"

"There is a great sickness in my heart, Johnny," he told me. "Come with me into the lodge of my father. We must talk."

I followed Antelope Foot into the tepee of his father, Painted Bow. When I was inside, I saw what had happened. The body of Painted Bow lay on a blanket, the old warrior's face white with death. There were three bullet wounds in his chest and shoulder, and I fought back tears as I sat down beside my friend.

"How did this happen?" I asked, choking back a sob.

"Painted Bow and War Cloud ride the buffalo valleys in search of buffalo. They come upon long train of white man's wagons. These wagons far south of trail. Painted Bow ride to tell white men this. They shoot, kill. War Cloud also die. Now valley stained with much blood. Little Deer, Dancing Willow, Two Horn all dead. Many white men die."

"The Sioux attacked the wagon train?" I asked.

"These white men came to our lands," Antelope Foot said, anger in his voice. "They take lives of Sioux warriors. We fight wagons, kill white men."

"And the women and children?" I asked.

"We kill all," Antelope Foot said, his voice calm and deadly.

"The soldiers will come," I said.

"No soldier will come," Antelope Foot said. "You see fort. Only children at fort. Officers all old and lame. It not day for war to come."

"And will the Sioux now fight the fort?" I asked. "Will they kill more white men?"

"There are those who would do so," Antelope Foot said. "There are those like Snake Nose who would strike you down this moment. But the whites who have killed my father will kill no more. There will be no war."

"I'm glad to hear this," I said. "I feel too deeply for you, Antelope Foot, to think of this as a time of war between us. I lost my father, too, and my heart is full of pain for your loss."

"I see your heart always in your eyes, Johnny," he said.

"You are always true to your heart, more Sioux than white man. I understand what is within you, what you are. It is your people I do not understand."

"My people?" I asked. "You have known Trader Jim longer than I have."

"I mean the white people," he said sadly. "They come as locusts. The Sioux have hunted these lands forever. Now we are told this is to be no more. Great snakes of wagons cross the buffalo valleys, muddy the clear streams, kill our game. These are not people."

"Not people?" I asked.

"They are devils with white skins. Devils with arms and legs. They kill the buffalo for his hide, leaving the meat that would keep the children's eyes bright through the winters to rot in the summer sun. They kill our people because they have red skins. No man does such things. No being with a heart can have such anger in his eyes."

"I don't understand that myself," I said. "I've been raised in a land where greed is a way of life. But all my life I've looked up to honor and courage as the only way a man can live his life. I'm confused by this. I fear I'll never understand how the two can exist in the same world."

"Will these white men change?" Antelope Foot asked me. "Will they set aside this hunger for the lands of the Sioux? Will they learn as you have to live with us, hunt in our way, love the land as we do?"

"I don't think so," I said. "Can the Sioux change?"

"For the Sioux to change would be for the Sioux to be the Sioux no more. My father once spoke to me of the mountains in this way. He said that the Sioux must be like the mountain. A mountain lives forever. It cannot be moved, for it belongs to the land, is a part of the earth. The Sioux are like this also."

"What will you do now?" I asked. "Will you come back to school?"

"I will come to the school no more," he said. "I am now a warrior. I will sit in my father's place in the council of the chiefs."

"Will I see you again?"

"This you will do," Antelope Foot said. "We are brothers, Johnny, and there is much you have yet to learn. I would share those things with you. We will hunt together in the mountains. This will come later. Would you walk with me to the place my father will be laid?"

"Will I be welcome there?" I asked. "I wouldn't want to be a reminder of the way Painted Bow died."

"You will be a reminder only that all white men are not devils."

"And Trader Jim? Is he also welcome?"

"The trader was a brother to my father," Antelope Foot said. "You will ride back and bring him. We will lay Painted Bow to rest as the sun is swallowed by the mountains."

"I will do it," I said. "I wish there were words for what is in my heart," I added, my eyelids growing heavy. "Painted Bow was always kind to me, and you have been the best friend I have ever known."

"You have been a brave friend, Johnny," he told me.

Then we clasped each other's arms and stood together for a moment. I wanted to say something, do something, but there was nothing to say or do. Everything was felt in that single moment, and I turned to go.

I rode on the wind back to Fort Laramie. When I told Trader Jim the news, he sat down and looked up at me with great sorrow on his face.

"I have lived too long," he told me. "I see all around me the companions of my youth killed off by the new ways of the world. Painted Bow was one of the last great warriors. The young ones don't ride with honor as their fathers did. They are too filled with hatred. They taste death, and it fills their hearts. A man should kill with regret, not with a smile on his face."

"Will you ride with me to the burial?" I asked him.

"Yes, Johnny, I will come. This is a great honor Antelope Foot has extended to you, son. You will bear everything that happens with dignity?"

"Yes. Is there anything which must be done?" I asked.

"We will take Painted Bow a present for his journey into the world beyond the stars. A buffalo gun," Trader Jim said, walking over to a shelf and taking down a new rifle. "This is the best we have. It is a fit thing."

We rode with Antelope Foot and the other Sioux into the mountains to the Sioux burial ground. There was a feeling in that place unlike any I'd ever known. The horses sensed something, and we had to leave them behind when we neared the burial site.

I walked beside Antelope Foot as he carried the body of his father. Painted Bow had been a large man, and Antelope Foot was not so much taller than me. But my friend carried his father as if the man had been a small child.

The Sioux did not bury their dead. They placed them on high wooden frameworks, wrapped in blankets. Their possessions were laid alongside them. As different warriors walked beside Painted Bow, I watched them place presents beside his body. Trader Jim laid the great buffalo gun there, and many of the Sioux looked at us differently.

I chased a tear from my eye as Antelope Foot walked up at last and placed beside his father the treasured bow, painted with all the colors of the earth and sky. Then the Sioux chanted their mournful words, and sadness settled over all of us.

There was something else there, too, though. It was a presence I had never felt before. The wind whispered through the trees, and the skies stirred. The sun was finally swallowed by the mountains, and the day was gone.

"The days of Painted Bow, my brother, are no more," Trader Jim sighed. "I wish him well in the next world."

One by one the Sioux walked away from the burial scaffold. Trader Jim motioned more than once for me to go, but I stayed until no one else was there. Trader Jim saw what I was doing and walked away.

"Antelope Foot, I don't know enough Sioux words to chant

like the others. But it seems like I should say something. I guess what I'd like to say is that Painted Bow was the kind of man my father was. He didn't run from danger. He loved his life, but he didn't fear his death. He was a man who will be missed."

"Would you walk with me this night, Johnny?" Antelope Foot asked me.

"I will do anything you would have me do," I said.

"Then come with me," he said, leading me away from the burial ground.

We sat down beside each other and looked out at the valley in the twilight. Silence filled the air, and we didn't stir. Then Antelope Foot turned to me.

"When your father die, Johnny, what did you do?"

"I cried," I told him. "I fought really hard not to, but there was nothing else to do. What do the Sioux do?"

"We cry also, but it is all inside," Antelope Foot said. "We mourn many moons for those who fall. But death is a part of life, and to find too many tears for one who is gone is to lose a part of life. There are never days enough in a man's life for some to be thrown away on one who is gone."

We spent most of the evening speaking of things we had done together. Then he turned to me and took my arm with his powerful wrist.

"Johnny, you are as much a brother to me as any my father could have given life. Know always that we two are as one, even if the wind sweeps everything we know away. The wind may change a man in many ways, but his heart must always keep a place for his brothers."

"Yes," I said. "That is the way it will always be with us."

As the air stirred with the chill of night, we separated. I returned to my mother and grandfather at the fort, and Antelope Foot went to his father's lodge, now his own. In the silence of the night I hoped and prayed that the winds of time would give us a few more years to be young, but I felt the breeze already stirring.

CHAPTER 9

The winds of change were kind to us. Seasons came and went, but the war clouds we all feared remained on the eastern horizon. The late spring of 1865 found us both strong and contented.

Antelope Foot and I hunted many times in the mountains. In the winters we journeyed north into the Powder River Valley to hunt deer and bighorn sheep. Once we made the trek to the mighty Missouri River, dodging scouts from Crow and Arikara hunting parties.

Antelope Foot spent the spring and summer outside the fort, living with a cluster of other Sioux who traded for guns and powder. It was the same type work we did, but Antelope Foot accepted only guns and ammunition for his wares.

Sometimes the two of us would ride down to the Platte to fish or swim on a lazy afternoon. There were buffalo hunts, too, and rare days of riding into the mountains.

In June the world changed. I walked in from a ride across the plains to find my mother busy making paper decorations.

"What are you doing?" I asked her. "Is someone having a birthday?"

"You haven't heard?" she asked me. "The war's over. The rebel generals have all surrendered. The Union is whole again. Your father didn't die in vain."

"I'm glad," I said, trying to smile. "I wish we could live in a world without wars."

"Just don't say that tonight," she told me. "There's going to be a party at the colonel's house. Soldiers wouldn't care too much for a world without wars."

"Antelope Foot and Trader Jim think there will be more war with the Sioux when the wagon trains start bringing people out here."

"You've spent too much time with Indians," she said. "At the party, listen to the soldiers. The officers can tell you more about the future of the West than a hundred Sioux."

"Maybe," I said, frowning.

That night we all put on our finest clothes for the celebration. I put on my church coat and a new cotton shirt. Mother clipped my hair so that I looked like the model young gentleman. I would have been admitted to a presidential reception in Washington.

The celebration was really for the ladies. They danced with their husbands while Trader Jim and I watched. Then Mother pulled me over to one side and whispered in my ear.

"Why don't you go over and invite Pamela Ashworth to the dance floor?" she asked me.

"Mother, she's a foot taller than I am," I sighed.

One look into her eyes told me it had to be done, though. I led Pamela, daughter of Captain Ashworth, through the dance steps. It was like an ant trying to tow a lizard, and we soon gave it up. I was awkward, and Pamela was downright clumsy. She trampled my feet, and I thought I'd never walk again.

The officers spent most of the evening with Trader Jim around the punch bowl. They toasted General Grant, President Johnson, the armies, each other, even the Indians.

"Now we'll finally get some decent troops out here," said Captain Ashworth. "You're going to see some real changes. The government will quit playing around with the tribes. They'll start getting tough, like with the Arapaho in Colorado."

I frowned when he said that.

"The Sioux aren't the Arapaho, Captain," Trader Jim said. "If the Army is determined to have a war, the Sioux and Cheyenne will empty a lot of saddles. And in the end, no one will win."

"You're a romantic, Howard," the captain said. "The Indians are obsolete. Once the buffalo are gone, they will be, too. The United States of America needs the Indian lands for expansion. The railroads have to cross these spaces. Progress demands change."

"I wouldn't give a nickel for all your progress," Trader Jim said. "I've buried too many friends in these mountains to see factories and farms all over them."

"Times change, Howard," the colonel said, walking over. "But we still have treaties with the Indians. So long as they keep them, the Army will leave them alone."

Trader Jim smiled at the man and led me aside.

"Hear that, son?" he asked, laughing. "Since when? The Army hasn't kept any treaty it's made in my memory."

"Maybe things will change," I said.

"They will, but not that," he sighed.

I left the officers to their celebrating and my grandfather to his mourning. Slipping outside into the warm summer night, I walked back to the store. When I got there, Antelope Foot was waiting outside.

"I have waited for you, Johnny," he told me. "There is much being said. The mouths of the long knife soldiers are filled with words, but I do not know what to see in them."

"You've heard that the war back East is over?" I asked.

"What does this mean?" he asked.

"I'm not sure," I said. "The colonel says the treaties will be kept, but Trader Jim laughed at that. One thing is for sure. There's an army of two hundred thousand men back East with no one to fight."

"I have not heard of such a number," Antelope Foot said. "How many men is that?"

"There are about five hundred men in a full cavalry regiment, Antelope Foot," I explained. "This would make four hundred regiments like that."

"Four hundred?" he asked. "This means the long knife will come like the buffalo. If a Sioux kills three of these, there will be ten more to take their place. The Sioux cannot kill so many men."

"Then the Sioux must keep the peace," I said. "You can speak to your council."

"This would be a thing for a great chief, but I speak in the council with a small voice. I also hear my father's words ring in my ears. The Sioux must be like the mountain. No mountain can move."

"And when the people come again?"

"Things will be as they must be. The long knife soldier is like a hungry wolf. When such a wolf finds no sheep to fill his belly, then that wolf will hunt other game. Long knife no longer have other long knife to fight. He turn to Sioux."

"And what about us?" I asked.

"Is easy for me," he said. "I Sioux warrior. I fight and die. You have great trial to face. Must come with Sioux where spirit is or stand with white people you born to."

"I don't know what to do," I said. "I used to dream of being a soldier. But if I become a soldier, it would be to fight the Indian. I couldn't fight a people I understand better than my own."

"You have much sadness in your eyes, my brother," he said. "The winds of battle have not blown across our path yet. Would you ride with me to the mountains this night?"

"At night?" I asked. "You wish to ride into the mountains at night? We've never tried to do this before. Do you trust your life to me, Antelope Foot?"

"My brother, I hold your heart in mine. I trust you as I trust no other man. The courage and honor that grows inside you touches all that know you. We will hunt bear perhaps. We will come to know each other and the land in a way your colonel could never understand."

"I'm not as strong or as tall as you, Antelope Foot, but if you trust me, I will be your companion. Let me leave a note for my mother and grandfather. Then we will seek the mountains."

I left the note and changed my clothes. Then I saddled my horse and followed my friend into the night. There was a great feeling of adventure in the summer air, and I looked forward to proving my manhood.

CHAPTER 10

We hunted the mountain for three days. It was not serious hunting, but we did kill some rabbits for food. We hunted more for sport, and we looked for signs of panther or bear tracks. We found none, and we laughed that it was probably as well. Any full-grown panther or bear could have made short work of the both of us.

On our third day out, we picked up deer tracks, and we set off after the game.

"I'm very tired of rabbit, Antelope Foot," I said. "We could kill a deer and have a feast."

"Deer not much of manhood test," he said, frowning. "I hope we kill bear or cougar."

"That may be," I said. "But it would fill my stomach and give new power to my legs to eat from a deer."

"Then we kill deer, Johnny," Antelope Foot told me.

We set out in the morning on foot, fearing the horses would only serve to reveal our presence. The tracks grew fresher upstream from our camp, and we began there. We walked softly through the mountain meadows, circling around so that the wind blew into our faces. This would prevent the animals from picking up our scents.

As we waited for the deer to approach our position, I watched the calm that filled Antelope Foot's face. He was relaxed, perfectly at peace with the world. It was a thing he understood. His people survived because he and other warriors hunted animals for food and clothing.

"There," I whispered to him, pointing to three deer coming into a small clearing. "I will aim at the buck on the right."

"I take buck in middle, "Antelope Foot said.

We waited several minutes before aiming. Then we leveled our rifles and fired. Both deer went down instantly, and the third bolted. Our aim had been good, for when we walked to the animals, we found both of them dead where they had fallen.

"We kill many deer, Johnny," Antelope Foot said to me. "We shoot straight."

"Yes," I said, smiling at him. "Now we have to take the deer back to camp and clean them."

"This night we eat much," Antelope Foot said, rubbing his naked stomach. "We eat like warriors."

We dragged the deer back to our camp and set to work dressing them. The knife I'd been given by Black Kettle was sharp and very effective for skinning. I gutted the deer and started skinning them while Antelope Foot began carving up the meat.

We built a great fire that night and roasted the deer in a bed of coals. We dug up some wild onions and turnips to complete our dinner, feasting until nightfall.

When the sun went down, we pulled our blankets close to the fire and prepared for bed. Antelope Foot lay on one side of the fire while I lay on the other. The uneaten venison and the carcasses we placed on a scaffold to keep the animals away. Then we went to bed.

As I was beginning to surrender to a peaceful sleep, a strange sound filled the air. It was more than a growl, but not quite a roar. I sat up, but Antelope Foot was on his feet in a flash. He ran for his rifle, but something flashed through the moonlight, and he withdrew.

I shook myself awake and reached for the pistol I'd brought with me from the store. I took it in my right hand and stood up.

"Johnny!" Antelope Foot yelled. "Cougar!"

The creature growled deeply, then circled the fire so as to have me in plain sight. I saw only a shadow in the night, but I sensed it was climbing the tree overlooking our camp.

"Johnny, it in tree!" Antelope Foot called out to me, waving his knife to my left.

The cougar growled angrily, then raced up the branch and dove through the air at me. In the instant of time I had to think, I moved the barrel of the pistol in front of me and fired rapidly three times. Two of my bullets tore into the beast, but it didn't stop. My shoulder burned with pain as its claws ripped through my shirt and dug into the soft flesh of my chest.

"Antelope Foot!" I cried out.

But before I could hear anything, a throb filled my head, and I collapsed.

I woke minutes later as Antelope Foot splashed water on my face. Great worry filled the face of my friend.

"I'm all right," I said, trying to rise.

That was when I realized my shirt was soaked with blood. The cougar had slashed deeply.

"How long?" I asked.

"Do not speak," he told me. "You bleed much, but I make you well. You brave man, never cry out."

My eyes were cloudy, but looking to my right side, I could see the cougar's dead body stretched out beside me.

"You killed the cougar," I said softly.

"You do that, Johnny," he said to me. "You kill with gun. He mark you with look of death upon his eyes."

Antelope Foot took out his knife and cut away my shirt. The blood still flowed, but Antelope Foot placed a wet cloth against the wound and pressed down hard.

"You have good scar from this night," Antelope Foot said. "You tell many stories of this night."

"I think I'd rather have a new chest," I told him.

"Pain pass soon. You be better tomorrow, Johnny."

I lay down quietly and let Antelope Foot tend my wound. He soon had the bleeding stopped.

"We mend this soon," he said. "Pain may come now. I give you stick to bite."

He placed a twig in my mouth, then reached back and grabbed my belt. Then he tugged me toward the river.

The pain worked its way through my shoulder and chest, and I bit down hard on the stick. When I finally reached the stream, Antelope Foot tore a strip of cloth from the back of my bloody shirt and soaked it in the river.

"I clean wound, my brother. Soon it be better."

He washed my neck and chest carefully, then brushed back the hair from my forehead. He finally cleaned the blood from the wound itself, opening it again.

"This hurt very much I think," he said, frowning. "I bring knife through fire. This burn out evil odors from wound. It hurt much, but must be done."

"Do it," I said, feeling the life flow out of me as the blood ran down my stomach.

Antelope Foot returned with his knife red hot. Then he pressed the knife against my chest, and it burned through my whole being. I bit down hard on the stick until it snapped in two. Then I passed out.

I came back to consciousness the next morning. I was lying bare-chested on my blankets, my head dizzy from loss of blood. The wound on my chest was clean and already on the mend. I ran my fingers along the tender flesh.

"You have great scar below neck," Antelope Foot told me.

I saw that his eyes no longer held the fear and worry of the night before.

"You saved my life," I told him. "I would have bled to death."

"You save my life, Johnny," he told me. "Cougar kill me if you not shoot it. I have only knife to fight with."

"Then we're even," I told him. "What do we do now?"

"You do nothing," he said. "Rest. I tend to you."

"How long will it be before I can ride?" I asked.

"Three, maybe four day. You be better soon."

The days passed quickly. Venison helped mend my torn body, and Antelope Foot worked the deerskins. He skinned the cougar, too, making a vest of its hide. He also had a new buckskin shirt ready for me.

He separated the cougar claws, bringing them to me the night before we planned to return to Fort Laramie.

"You search for name all of time you ride the buffalo valleys," Antelope Foot said. "You hunt and trade, but only now you get your name. Just as Crow give my father the painted bow, this cougar give you mark of warrior. These claws give you name. You now be Cougar Claw to me always. I make necklace for you of these claws."

"Make two necklaces," I told him. "Split them between us. The claws will bind us together, just as this adventure has. That way no matter where we are or what we do, we'll always be bound to each other."

"This I will do," he said. "We ride to fort in morning. We leave as boys, but we ride back as men. We always men from this day. We brothers. We share night of cougar's death. We share danger. This binds man more than necklace of cougar claws."

"Yes," I agreed. "But the claws will always remind me."

With the coming of morning, we rode back to the fort. It was a long journey, but we rode fast, eager to tell everyone of our adventure. I rode taller than before in the saddle, a new confidence filling my insides.

CHAPTER 11

When Antelope Foot and I reached the fort, he pulled his pony to a halt.

"Cougar Claw, my brother, I leave you," he told me. "You are strong enough to go on?"

"Yes," I said. "Will you come with me?"

"I must find my own lodge," Antelope Foot said. "You will see me when scars heal."

I left him outside the fort, riding past the sentry alone. I was tired, and my face was white with weakness, but I managed to stable my mustang and stagger inside the little house behind the store.

I opened the door quietly, trying to conceal my entrance from Mother. Trader Jim, though, rushed into the front room, smiling as his eyes fell on me.

"Son, we been expecting you back for a couple of days now," he said to me. "You look a might sickly."

"I've had a great adventure," I said.

"You can tell me all about it tomorrow. You've come a long ways. I can see it written on your face. Let me help you to your bed."

"I can make it," I said, struggling forward.

Trader Jim wrapped his arm around me and shifted my weight to his shoulders. There was something comforting about the firmness in those shoulders of his, and I leaned on him.

When we got into the storeroom, Trader Jim helped me to a bench, then spread out some blankets for me on my pine slat bed.

"What's this you got around your neck?" he asked me.

"Cougar claws," I said. "I shot a cougar on the mountain."

"That's no easy thing to do," he said. "Cougar's just about the most slippery animal there is. Let's see here," he said, slipping his fingers along my neck to feel the necklace.

His bright eyes lost their glow, though, as he saw the bandage on my chest.

"What's this?" he asked me. "Boy, you're hurt!"

"It's just about healed," I said.

"Get your shirt off. Let's see," he told me.

I winced with pain as I slid the deerskin shirt over my shoulders. Then I peeled the cotton undershirt down to my waist.

"It's bled some," Trader Jim told me. "Let's get some water. We'll have to soak it. I'm goin' to send for the post doctor."

"Don't tell Mother," I pleaded. "She'll just get all upset."

"I have to," he said. "I want her to fetch the doctor."

I frowned heavily, but he brushed back a strand of hair from my eyes with a comforting smile.

"She'll holler a little, but it's just out of love, son. She's missed you these last few days. I thought that woman was goin' to go crazy."

Trader Jim left me alone in the storeroom. A moment later he returned with my mother. In his hands was a basin of water and two clean cloths.

"Johnny, you're hurt," Mother said, sitting beside me. "What happened?"

"A cougar attacked our camp," I explained. "I shot it, but it tore into me with its last breath. The wound is deep, but we kept it clean."

"Woman, dry your tears," Trader Jim told her as she started crying. "Go get Doc Stratton. By the time you get him down here, I'll have the bandages off."

Mother gave me a parting look, then left the room on her way to get the doctor. Trader Jim set to work on the bandages.

I winced as he soaked the soft cotton away from the wound.

Then he pulled the last of it from the charred flesh that had been broken by the cougar's claws.

"You were in good hands on that mountain, son," he told me. "Antelope Foot did a fine job cleaning this wound. It will heal up just fine."

"He is a good friend," I said. "All the time I was hurt he kept telling me how brave I was, how proud you'd be that I killed the cougar. And all that time I was scared to death."

"That's the way of the Sioux," Trader Jim said, smiling. "They don't know what fear is. They are a brave people."

"Yes," I said. "He gave me a Sioux name, too. Cougar Claw. It's a fitting name. I'm going to carry the scars that cougar gave me as long as I live."

"To carry a scar you receive in a cowardly act is one thing, son," Trader Jim said. "But to carry a scar got in an act of courage is like one of those medals your father wore on his uniform. Wherever you go, those scars will remind you of who you are and what you have been."

"I will never need to be reminded of that," I said.

"I see that in your eyes, son. But men change as they grow up. Your life is ahead of you, and it may not lie here in the West as mine has."

"I'd like my life to always be here," I said. "I belong here with you and Antelope Foot and the mountains and rivers and prairies."

"You are mostly a man now, Johnny," he said. "As long as I'm here, there'll be a place for you if you want it."

He sat down beside me on the bed, and I leaned my head against his shoulder. I knew men really didn't lean on people, but for some reason I had a sudden urge to lean my head back on my grandfather's shoulder the same way I'd leaned on my father's shoulder when I was little.

Mother walked in with Dr. Stratton soon afterward, and she smiled at me. I suppose that leaning on Trader Jim I looked less like a man.

The doctor probed and poked me some, then smiled.

"The wound is clean," he said. "Should heal up just fine."

"Is there anything special he should do?" Mother asked.

"I'd get some sun to that flesh," the doctor said. "The skin's so white I thought it might belong to a ghost. Just get out in the sun some. Shouldn't be too hard for a boy to do in the summer."

"No, sir," I said.

Trader Jim walked the doctor out of the room, and Mother helped me to my bed. Then she walked away, too, and I was left alone in the silence of the storeroom.

I slept well in my warm bed that night. The chill of the mountains was forgotten, and I dreamed of all kinds of adventures I would share with Antelope Foot.

When my eyes greeted the morning, I discovered that I was a celebrity. Trader Jim had spread word of my scars, and Antelope Foot had told the Sioux warriors of our adventure. I found myself sitting on the sunny porch of the store relating the whole story.

"I have heard of such things," spoke Beaver Belt, one of the Sioux traders. "It is said that a man who is marked by the cougar can be saved only by the spirits. The spirits must be pleased with you, Cougar Claw."

My grandfather celebrated my courage for a week. He took out the whiskey jug and shared a drink with anyone who would oblige him.

Mother's attitude was quite different. She hadn't really been happy since I'd gotten back, but the more I talked about my adventure, the more unhappy she got. One afternoon when I came in from a fishing outing with Antelope Foot, she pulled me aside and led the way to her room.

"Johnny, I want to talk to you," she said, sitting down in a chair.

"I'm always ready to talk to you," I said, smiling. "Would you like to call me Cougar Claw like everyone else?"

"That's what I want to talk to you about," she said. "You were born John Whitlock. It was your father's name, a respected name. You can take that name anywhere, and people will look up to it."

"I know that," I said. "I've always been proud of it."

"All this Cougar Claw nonsense. You're getting as bad as your grandfather."

"As bad as my grandfather?" I asked. "Bad about what? There's nothing wrong with Trader Jim."

"Not ten years ago," she said. "But it's not 1855. Your grandfather will never change. He's an old man whose world has outgrown him. He tries to fool himself, but he can't be the wild man of the mountains anymore. He has to be a poor trader in a little fort in the middle of nowhere."

"You never talked like this when we came out here," I said. "He's given us a home, and he's been a father to me. I love him, and I love his world. I've learned more about courage and honor than I could have in a hundred of Grandmother Whitlock's fancy Pennsylvania military schools."

"There's more to life than courage and honor," she said. "There's business. You can read and do figures, but you have to learn how to deal with people in polite society."

"Why?" I asked. "I don't have any use for all those little napkins and tiny forks and such."

"You will, Johnny. Your grandmother won't live forever. She'll leave you a great deal of money. I've saved some myself. This fall I'm sending you to your grandmother. That way you can learn from her what you will need to know."

"I won't go," I said. "I'll never go."

"Look, Johnny," she said, "you're nearly a man. You don't look it on the outside yet, but to listen to you is to hear the words, the feelings of a man. You can't go around acting like a wild Indian."

"That's the life I understand, Mother," I said. "It's what I choose to be."

"Look, Johnny, your grandfather has become a man lost in the past. He'll never understand the future that's coming. You must be a man for the future."

"I'll try," I said. "I'll work as hard as you say with books, with figures, with anything you say. But I'm staying in Laramie. Trader Jim says there's a place here for me as long as I want it, and I want it. For me, the only things that matter are the mountains and the rivers and the prairies. It may not stay this way for long. There may be wars and death all around us soon, but right now I have to spend my moments with Antelope Foot. He's the only brother I've ever known. I don't know how to explain how I feel, Mother, but I can't leave."

"I've lost you, Johnny," she sighed. "I never should have brought you here. It was a mistake."

She looked at me for a moment. Then she gave me a big hug and a kiss. Her eyes were full of defeat, and as I left her, I felt I left a part of me behind, too.

CHAPTER 12

A year came and went, and I grew taller.

My legs were powerful now, and I could run with the wind. My shoulders and arms had a new power, too, and I fought with a knife or a lance or a saber as well as any man in the fort. I outran Antelope Foot, but he was still more than my equal with a knife or a lance.

If I'd proven my courage on a summer night a year before, I had proven in the last year that I had the cleverness, the quickness of mind, to deal with all manner of people. During the summer I rode alone to the camps of the Cheyenne, Sioux, and Arapaho with trade goods. But I found few Arapaho and Cheyenne. Only the Sioux still camped near the Platte.

Much had changed in the year since the war had ended. More white people had left the battle-scarred East to find new beginnings in the West. The people who came never saw the mountains and the rivers I loved. Their eyes were on the distant mountains and golden fields of California and Oregon.

They lacked understanding, too. They rode with anger in their eyes, and they fought because they didn't know the joy of life. They fought because it was easier for them than understanding. Many Sioux and Cheyenne and Arapaho died that summer, swept away by the winds of change those white men brought with them.

I was troubled by the changes that came with the wagons. Laramie was growing, and civilization was arriving. The day when the lands were covered with buffalo had passed, and I came to look forward to the few times I went into the mountains with Antelope Foot to hunt deer.

During the summer of 1866, my fifteenth on this earth, my eyes came to see the one thing I had long feared. In the middle of June a long column of soldiers rode within sight of Fort Laramie.

They carried shiny new rifles which fired many times without reloading. They pulled long cannons which could in a single flash carry out more destruction than ten of the best Sioux warriors. I had long feared the coming of the Army, and now they were here.

These men were commanded by a Colonel Carrington, a veteran of the war in the East.

It was not a good time for me. Red Cloud, great chief of the Sioux, had brought a thousand of his people to the fort. There were a thousand others there already, mostly Sioux and Cheyenne. They were gathered to hear the words of a treaty commissioner, and the arrival of seven hundred soldiers caused much alarm.

The soldiers at the fort grew nervous. They made a great show of firing off the cannons to show the thunder they commanded. Indians who had walked unarmed into Trader Jim's store a hundred times before now brought their rifles and war lances when they came. There was much talk of battle among the young men in the Sioux camps.

I was puzzled by all the words of war among the Indians and the soldiers. Nobody wanted war, but everyone seemed willing to see it happen. I listened to the colonels at the fort talk about how they wanted a new treaty. I listened to Sioux warriors complain of the white man's breaking of the old treaty. But the white men had promised presents to Red Cloud, had given him powder and shot. And the Indians were there at the fort. They were not hiding in ambush or raiding the wagon trains.

Whenever I was worried about things the way I was now, I always rode out to the Sioux camp to talk to Antelope Foot. I could trust the truth in his words. With the Sioux camped beside the fort, I walked the short distance to his lodge.

Antelope Foot had grown as tall as his father had been, and

he looked down on me as always. It didn't seem to bother him that I was smaller, and I didn't mind looking up to him. I found him in front of his lodge, cleaning a new rifle he had bought in the spring.

"Getting ready for battle?" I asked him.

"I hope no battle come, Cougar Claw," he said.

"What will Red Cloud do?" I asked him.

"Red Cloud know that. Spirits of mountains know that. I not know what Red Cloud do. But Red Cloud like my father. He say Sioux like the mountain. Red Cloud not sell hunting grounds of Sioux. We have treaty. If white man break treaty, we fight."

"Have you seen all the soldiers?" I asked. "Have the Sioux heard the big guns?"

"Guns may speak thunder, but they not go where Sioux go. Sioux fight like the wind. Here, there, everywhere. Long knife not see, not shoot, not kill what not see or shoot."

"You know more than I'll ever know about the Sioux," I told him. "But I know the long knife soldiers. I grew up with them before I ever came here. These men don't fight like the Sioux."

"They fight without honor?"

"They fight with their own kind of honor," I said. "They fight without bothering to understand their enemy. The Sioux have to understand their enemy before they can go to battle with him. But the blue-coat soldiers only understand what they are told to do. If they are told to shoot, they shoot. If they are told to ride, they ride."

"They do not fight with skill, with cunning. We kill them very easy."

"No, Antelope Foot. They fight as one man with many eyes, many hands. You can't defeat him because every time you shoot a hand or an eye, he grows another."

I didn't speak with Antelope Foot again for many days. Colonel Carrington's men brought needed supplies, and I was hired by the soldiers to help keep accounts in the warehouse.

I had done this many times, but it bothered me that I would be shut away in a warehouse while so much was going on.

When the stores were all recorded, the reason for Colonel Carrington's arrival became known. He had brought soldiers to build a road through the Powder River Valley. The news brought a shudder to my whole being. The Sioux would never stand for a road through their last great hunting grounds. The trail along the Platte had ruined the buffalo hunting. The white man's roads were splitting the great tribes into little clusters and villages.

Once again I went to see Antelope Foot. Red Cloud had turned down the offer of a new treaty, and the camps of the Sioux and Cheyenne were breaking up. I found Antelope Foot preparing to leave with a band of warriors.

"I would speak with you, Antelope Foot," I said. "Have you time?"

"This is bad day for us, Cougar Claw," he said. "I go now to wait for the clouds of war."

"That is why I must talk to you," I said.

"Yes, it is so," he said, looking seriously into my eyes. "I never know anything but truth and honor in those eyes, Cougar Claw. I move my lodge with Red Cloud, but I go this night to burial place of my father. Would you ride with me to this place of spirits? It may be that you will have answers for these questions."

I returned to the fort and saddled my horse. Then I quietly made my way to where Antelope Foot was waiting. We rode in silence to the mountain where Painted Bow's bones rested on their burial scaffold.

The place was deathly still, and I felt my bones tremble. But Antelope Foot was calm as always, and I followed him step for step. When we reached the scaffold of his father, I watched him sit down beside it. I recognized the painted bow the Crow chief had given the old warrior. Then I sat down beside my friend and waited for sleep to come.

Antelope Foot expected a vision, but none came to either of us. I felt myself filled with a greater peace, though, and when we camped the next morning on the mountainside, it was like old times.

"We came up here once to hunt bear," I said to him. "We could do that again. I'm stronger than before, and you're as tall and strong as your father."

"That would be a fine hunt, Cougar Claw," he said. "But the time for hunting bear with you, my brother, is past. I go today to fight the white chief Carrington. He would build forts on the land of the Sioux. He would drive away the deer with a road for wagons."

"Why do you suppose we have to fight each other, Antelope Foot? All men are the same. We swam the river together as boys, hunted buffalo. You mended my torn flesh. Did it seem different from your own?"

"Your heart is as mine, Cougar Claw, but other white men do not see things. They close their eyes to the world. They see only yellow powder. They have hunger only for land. When there is no more land, they will kill other white men to get it. They do not hunt the land. They do not respect the land. They only understand killing."

"They will kill our world," I told him.

"They do that this day," he said. "Even as we sit in council, Eagle Chief Carrington builds forts on our hunting grounds. Places where we walked in friendship white men will die this day in battle against the Sioux. This valley of the Powder River is last great hunting ground of Sioux. If we let the hand of the white man touch it, it will give birth to no more deer, no more elk, no more bighorn sheep. The Sioux will starve."

"When the day comes that you are gone, my brother, I will have lived too long."

"No man can call his own death to come," he said. "Change comes to my way of life. I mourn the passing of the buffalo as I mourned the passing of my father and my mother. But I will live on if it is commanded by the spirits."

As he spoke, a great cloud moved across the sun, casting darkness over us. Then a great blast of thunder boomed through the heavens.

"Listen to thunder, Cougar Claw," Antelope Foot said to me. "There are two kinds of thunder in the mountains. One kind comes to call the summer rains. It is gentle, cool. It brings the tall grasses. It brings back the buffalo."

"And the other?" I asked.

"It is angry, red with violence. It brings only the deep snows of winter. It brings death to the old and hunger to the young."

"And what kind is this?" I asked.

"It will bring the summer rains," he said. "But there is also the thunder of Eagle Chief Carrington. His thunder is angry. It is answered by the Sioux. Can you hear it, Cougar Claw? Can you hear the cry of my people? It is a cry of angry thunder. It will kill many white men before it is silent."

"But when it's silent . . ."

"The Sioux will be no more. But those who have heard the thunder, my brother, those like you who know of courage and honor; they will say to the ones who follow that the Sioux were a good people, a brave nation. Those who are left will remember that the Sioux died with honor."

When I rode away from him that day, I knew that we would never again sit together in council. The line which neither of us had ever drawn now separated us forever.

CHAPTER 13

Within a week the clouds of war had settled into the Powder River Valley. Colonel Carrington's infantry regiment was building forts along the river, and the Sioux were raiding his supply wagons.

The Indians fought just as Antelope Foot had told me they would. The soldiers never saw them come, but they were always there. Every time a small party of soldiers went off to cut wood or bring in supplies, the Sioux attacked. But whenever the Indians launched an attack against a solid position, the soldiers used their repeating rifles to chop the Indian masses into shreds.

Whatever news reached Laramie brought sadness to me. Many of the soldiers in the field were old friends of mine from my growing up days at the fort. Some of the officers had served with my father. And whenever I heard of the death of a Sioux, I wondered if it had been my brother, Antelope Foot.

One night in that first week of the war, Trader Jim walked into the store with a great smile on his face.

"Johnny, have you ever heard me talk about my old friend Jim Bridger?" he asked me.

"Have I ever heard you talk about Jim Bridger?" I echoed his question. "I haven't heard much else since I've been here. You told me about the time you and Bridger trapped in the Wind River country. You even told me you were with him when he found the pass through the Rockies."

"Don't tell Big Jim that," he told me.

"Don't tell him?" I asked. "You mean he's here?"

"In Laramie," Trader Jim said. "He's scouting for Colonel

Carrington. He and a scout named John Crandell will be here tonight for dinner. Your mother's roasting a pig."

"Then there's a lot to look forward to," I said with a smile. "A feast as well as good company."

"The food will be delicious, son," he said. "As for the company, you may find three old men a bit too much to take. But, Johnny, when you speak to Jim Bridger, you speak to history itself."

To say that I was impressed by Crandell and Bridger would have been the greatest understatement imaginable. Not since meeting Black Kettle, chief of the southern Cheyenne, had I been so much in awe of other men.

Bridger was a mountain of a man, tall and weathered. Though he was now in his sixties, his eyes were sharp, and he seemed to look right through me. His shoulders and thighs were like iron, and I felt without knowing for sure that he could have taken on a whole platoon of the inexperienced soldiers in Carrington's command.

Crandell was a younger man. Smaller than Bridger, his eyes seemed to avoid me when I looked at him. There was something unsaid by his words that was transmitted by those strange eyes of his. It was as if he trusted no one. Worse, it seemed he was undeserving of trust himself. But since there was nothing for me to trust the man with, I didn't bother to concern myself with those deceitful eyes.

"Big Jim," my grandfather said to him, taking a weather-beaten hat from the old trapper, "it'd be my pleasure if you'd meet my grandson, Johnny Cougar Claw Whitlock."

"Boy, my pleasure to meet you," Bridger told me. "How'd you come by your name? I've an Indian name myself. Blanket Jim they call me."

"I got mine from a Sioux warrior," I said. "His name is Antelope Foot. He's the only brother I've ever had." Jim Bridger listened approvingly as I told him the cougar story. He seemed to accept me now on my own merits.

After dinner, Crandell, Bridger, and Trader Jim walked out to the porch and sat down in the soft summer breeze. I walked out and joined them, listening to their countless tales of adventure and romance in the early days of the American West. There were great Indian battles, cold winters, narrow escapes from raging fires and wild animals. By the time the night chill was upon us, we were all tired and ready for sleep.

"Big Jim," my grandfather said, "what do you think about Carrington's campaign against Red Cloud?"

"Carrington's got the men, the supplies, the big guns, and the repeating rifles. His forts will never be taken. But Carrington will never win unless Red Cloud attacks the forts. Those Sioux chop away at his supply trains. His scouting parties get ambushed every time they go out. Carrington's men are a mixture of galvanized Yankees and eastern slum rats. The first bunch don't have their heart in the fight, and the others can't soldier any better than they can do anything else."

"They die well, though," Crandell said. "I seen a patrol mow down twenty Sioux before they got themselves overrun. They ain't scared of fighting. They just get led poorly."

"Say, Johnny," Bridger said to me, "what do you do here anyway?"

"I keep books for Trader Jim," I said. "I go to school some, and I help out at the warehouse sometimes."

"Not much of a life for a cougar killer, huh, Crandell?" Bridger asked. "How'd you like to come out with us?" he asked me.

"I don't know," I said. "I have many friends among the Sioux. I wouldn't want to bring about their death."

"Boy, the Sioux *are* dead," Crandell said. "If Red Cloud can hold off Carrington, all it means is some other soldier will come out here and wipe them Indians out later. A young fellow like you could make a mark as an army scout. Today is a good time to fight with the Army. Tomorrow may be too late."

"Too late for who?" I asked.

"Too late for any of us," Bridger said. "The West is a different place every year now. You got to grow with it or die. The Sioux never will change."

"A mountain can't change," I said. "It stands for all time in its beauty."

"Funny thing about mountains, son," Bridger said. "I seen mountains that men put holes plum through. I saw mountains that got themselves chopped into little hills."

"Would I really be useful?" I asked.

"A boy who knows the Powder River will be like an extra pair of eyes," Crandell said. "Do you speak the language of the Sioux?"

"I can speak with Sioux, Cheyenne, Arapaho, and Arikara," I said. "I can speak with the Sioux almost like a member of the tribe. I'm known to them."

"So am I," Bridger said. "Johnny, if you come with us, remember to never fall captive to the Indians. They'd hack you to pieces. You take great care."

"I will," I said.

I searched my heart long and hard. I didn't like the feelings I had for the soldiers, but I couldn't stand being left out of something which would shape my world.

I spoke to Colonel Carrington the next day. He refused to let me scout for him, but he agreed to take me along to help tend the horses. I knew horses as well as any man alive, and it eased my mind to know I wouldn't be really fighting against the Sioux.

Mother argued against my plans. She didn't want a son scalped by the Sioux. But I was no longer a boy, and I went anyway.

The days ahead were destined to challenge the best that was within me. I would be pushed to the limit of physical and emotional endurance. But I knew challenges well, and I had to face the world on its own terms, not hide away in the store when the West was changing before my very eyes.

CHAPTER 14

I rode the rest of the summer with the Army. I tended horses, mended harness, and carried messages for Colonel Carrington and the other officers. I held a strange place among the soldiers. In a way, my youth made me a younger brother to many of them. But once the troopers learned that I knew the land and the Indians, they came to ask me a hundred questions.

It was a strange array that filled the ranks of Colonel Carrington's command. There was a core of regular army men, veterans of the Indian campaigns of the 1850s and the war against the South. The others were mostly Union soldiers who'd stayed in the Army after the war.

The oddest group were the galvanized Yankees, men who had agreed to serve under the Union flag in order to be released from federal prisoner-of-war camps. Those men hated the others and kept to themselves. They cursed the officers, cursed the Indians, cursed the Army, the food, the weather. But they fought with great courage.

Colonel Carrington garrisoned the small fort on the Powder River with these galvanized Yankees. It was good that these former rebels had courage, for there was need of it. The Sioux cut off this fort from supplies, and many a southern boy who had survived the Wilderness and Fredericksburg starved in the little stockades beside the Powder River.

My responsibilities were with the horses, so I often made the trip with supplies to the little fort. The supply trains were always attacked, and more than once I saw men die on the coulees. On our next trip out we would find the bodies where they fell, stripped naked, face down in the buffalo grass.

The Sioux, those few who were killed, were taken away by their fellow warriors. The army soldiers, though, died where they fell. Those who were left still alive suffered terrible tortures. All were scalped.

I had seen many things in my lifetime, but I will never forget the horror that filled my heart when I saw my first scalped soldier. There is no more hideous sight imaginable. The sight of the young man, his naked body bleached by the summer sun, was like something out of a nightmare. His eyes were frozen open, a look of astonishment fixed upon his face.

It was that look of surprise that terrified me. I suppose it was the way with death at a young age. It was never expected, and the fact that it had happened to that young soldier simply proved that it could also happen to me.

We buried many soldiers on our supply missions, but we never reached the fort. Only when the colonel mustered a big escort did the supply wagons get through.

In the evenings I sat around the campfires and listened to the soldiers speak of home. There were some from Pennsylvania, and they spoke of the cities, the grand houses, the rolling countryside I remembered from my past in the other world of the East. I never spoke when they talked and sang and laughed about their homes. It was a world foreign to me now.

I remembered what Trader Jim had said about these men. He'd said they came from a different world. Antelope Foot had said often they came into the lands of the Sioux without reverence, without understanding. It was true. The soldiers didn't understand why the Sioux fought. Or *how* they fought.

The Sioux came from nowhere to strike at the most vulnerable spot in the Army's defense. Their attacks were always unexpected and usually successful. But it was not always so.

I sat around the campfire one night as a tall corporal joined us, his eyes full of excitement. His mouth broadened into a wicked smile. Then he spoke.

"We got a piece of them Sioux this morning, boys," he said. "Old bucks thought they had us by surprise down by the river cutting wood, but Captain Ballman got us to cover. We got them repeaters spitting lead into them Indians, and we stitched a few bellies. Why you could have walked fifty yards over nothing but dead bucks."

"Billy," another soldier said, "you should have seen them Sioux fighting each other over who could get himself killed. I thought them bucks was going to shoot themselves if they didn't get their ticket to the happy hunting ground."

The soldiers went on to describe the dying agonies of proud Sioux warriors, and I winced in pain. Some of the deaths they had brought that morning came to men I had camped with, hunted with, grown up with. I wanted to walk away from the fire and be alone, but the soldiers wouldn't have understood.

"You should have seen this one buck," the corporal said. "He rode around just out of range, waving us to him. There he was, one Sioux all alone."

"That's an old Sioux trick," I said, surprised that I'd spoken.

"What's that?" a soldier asked. "What kind of trick?"

"That's the way the Sioux fight," I said. "Hit and run. If you'd ridden after that one man, you'd have found fifty come from nowhere to ambush you."

"How'd you know that, boy?" the corporal asked me.

"I've seen the Sioux many times," I told them. "They would fight you hand to hand, but that isn't your way. They know you can stand behind cover with your repeating rifles and cut them to pieces, so they lead you into ambush where they can strike like lightning."

"You like them Indians, boy?" the corporal growled. "Maybe you like them better than us, huh? Maybe you trade a little with the Sioux. How many soldier boys lie dead out there 'cause of you?"

"None," I said, standing up. "I've never hidden from the Sioux. I've shared every danger with you. My father died at Manassas wearing the same uniform you do. I know the Sioux.

I understand them. That doesn't mean I'm a coward or a traitor!"

They said nothing for several minutes. Then they settled back to their songs of home. But it was understood how it was with me after that. I was no ally of the Sioux, but I didn't share the soldiers' joy in killing them, either.

That winter I served under Colonel Carrington at Fort Phil Kearney on the forks of Piney Creek.

One day as I was tending horses, Colonel Carrington himself rode up to me and dismounted.

"Johnny," he said, "I hear you know this country well."

"Yes, sir," I said. "I've hunted here often with my brothers, the Sioux."

"Brothers?" he asked.

"It's a word people here use to show understanding, friendship," I said.

"Well, son, for what I have in my mind, I wouldn't be wanting a brother of the Sioux at my side. I'd want a man who could fight his way through fire."

"You'd find I could do that for the right reason," I told him. "I'm my father's son, and I understand loyalty. I can follow orders, too."

"Could you kill a Sioux?" he asked me.

"I'll tell you the truth," I said. "I've never killed a man, but I'd fight to save my life, or yours."

"You would, too," he said, smiling. "I have a problem. I sent Captain Fetterman down the trail, and I have reports he's engaged a large band of the enemy. Crandell and Bridger and my Indian scouts are all out. Could you lead a column through the valley safe from ambush?"

"I can get you down the valley," I said. "But I can't keep you from being attacked. I can warn you of the danger spots, but I've never done this sort of thing before. "

"But you know the Indians?" the colonel asked.

"Yes, sir," I said. "And I suppose I'm better than nothing at all."

"A good deal better, I'd wager," the colonel told me.

We rode a long time before we found signs of Fetterman's command. Soldiers clad in the bright blue uniforms of the Army lay scattered along the road where they had fallen. These soldiers still had their hair. It was clear they had fallen in the first minutes of the battle.

"What happened here?" the colonel asked.

"I think Fetterman chased a Sioux raiding party," I said. "They're in a running fight with the Sioux here."

"That can't be," the colonel said. "Fetterman was under orders not to go beyond Lodge Trail Ridge."

I swallowed deeply and looked at the colonel seriously.

"I could be wrong, sir," I said. "I haven't got much experience. But I'd say from what I know that the captain is probably fighting for his life up ahead somewhere."

"What?" the colonel asked. "Fetterman had two hundred men with him."

"That probably isn't enough," I told him. "Some of the arrows in these soldiers have Cheyenne and Arapaho markings."

"You sure?" he asked.

"Yes, sir," I said. "I've seen them many times."

"Then lead on, son," the colonel said.

We rode for some distance until we reached a hill. There we came upon a scene of utter horror. The buffalo grass ran red with blood. Bodies filled the rocky ground in heaps. Blue-coated soldiers lay shoulder to shoulder where they had met their deaths.

"Where are the survivors?" someone in the column asked.

I looked at Colonel Carrington.

"Are there any survivors, John?" the colonel asked me.

"I don't think there are," I said. "It looks like maybe a hundred bodies. A lot of Indians died here, too. They wouldn't let anyone get away."

It was a terrible sight. No sign of life came from the valley of death. Among the dead were Captain Fetterman and the old frontiersman, John Crandell. Many of the soldiers had been badly mutilated.

"What kind of devil could do a thing like this?" the colonel asked me. "What kind of man could hack his dead enemy apart like this? It's indecent."

My face was white, and my stomach rumbled. I had seen many things, but nothing compared to that. I climbed down from my horse, walking beside the terribly mauled bodies of the soldiers. The corporal who had boasted of the piles of Sioux bodies that had fallen before his repeating rifle did no boasting on that field. His rifle was nowhere to be found. His shirt had been torn open, and his bowels were spread out beside him.

My insides flamed, and I became sick. I vomited until I thought I would die. My head was light, and I stumbled away. Then I ran. I tried to escape the terror all around me, but I couldn't. I finally stopped beside my horse, plunging my head against my bare forearm. Then the tears streamed down my cheeks.

I hadn't thought there would ever again be tears from me for anyone or anything, but I'd been wrong. The death of two hundred men was more than I could take. The blood and the gore I'd seen in five minutes were more terrible than anything I'd seen in my most vivid nightmares.

I rode away with the column a different person, a man hardened to life in a new, different way. I was now a man who had lost his sense of purpose, direction. Most of all, I was afraid I would never again find that old understanding I had once known on a starry summer night in the Laramie Mountains.

CHAPTER 15

The war against Red Cloud and the Sioux changed after the Fetterman defeat. The eastern newspapers called the fight a massacre. They depicted the terrible atrocities performed on the bodies of the dead soldiers, calling the Sioux names like animal and dog. The editors urged the Army to wipe the Sioux from the face of the earth.

The soldiers wanted to do just that. A great thirst for revenge filled the ranks, and more than one soldier boasted of what he would do to the next Sioux man, woman, or child who came within his grasp.

The battle had a different effect on Colonel Carrington and General Conner, who was in command of the whole campaign. The commanders had more respect for the Sioux, and they kept the Army's exposure to attack minimal. I saw for myself that many of the officers who had sneered at the savage ignorance of the Sioux were now in utter fear of the Indians' determined resistance to the Army.

Within the Army there was a new call for a peaceful solution to the war, and a peace commission seemed to be in the wind. I prayed each night that orders would come which would call us back to Fort Laramie and out of the Powder River Valley. The land where I'd hunted deer and grown into self-reliance was now haunted by a nightmare of war and death.

I was a civilian, and I could have gone back to Laramie anytime. But I knew there would be questions I could never face if I did that. Going back meant accepting Mother's decisions, meant returning to Pennsylvania to live with Grandmother Whitlock. I wasn't desperate enough to admit defeat, to return to a world where I would be a boy once more. I'd paid too high a price for my manhood.

When the Army sent out a scouting party to locate the Sioux, I was assigned to go along. My scouting days were over. I went along to handle the horses.

We rode out through the heavy mist of a mountain morning. We soon crossed the river in our column of twos. I was in the rear with the supply wagons as we splashed through the river. Then we trotted away into the wild broken hill country that started past the coulees.

I'd ridden many times with the Army, but I sensed something different about this expedition. For one thing, we carried no stores bound for anyone. For another, the usual small talk that spread through the column was missing. The men were deadly serious, and there was a feeling of death around our little army.

Being in the rear of the column, I couldn't share the news the Arikara scouts brought of the country ahead. I could hear the stir of excitement that swept through the soldiers when Captain Carroll, our commander, issued orders.

It took many minutes for those orders to pass through the mouths of the soldiers all the way back to the supply wagons.

"We're riding against the Sioux, a whole village of them," the soldiers whispered. "For once we caught them napping."

A shiver wound itself through me. I knew no one ever rode upon the Sioux unseen or unheard. It would be the Fetterman scene all over again. Then an even worse thought entered my mind. We just might have come upon an undefended Sioux encampment filled with women and children and old people. A massacre would surely follow, and Red Cloud would never believe a peace commissioner when his people were being murdered in their camps.

At that moment, if I could have reached out and stopped what was destined to be, I would have. I'd have surrendered my very life to have ended the war at that moment. But it was not the way of things for a single man to have within his power the events of history, so what was to follow came to be.

The supply wagons were left some three hundred yards from the edge of the Sioux village. I stood beside my horse as the column of horsemen split in order to ride upon the camp from two directions. Captain Carroll mounted his attack as if he was drawing it on a classroom slate at the military academy at West Point.

I didn't share the soldiers' taste for revenge. While sabers flashed and Sioux died, I hid my eyes. In my ears the death cries of women will scream forever, never to be silenced. I trembled as I imagined the terror that filled the Sioux camp.

My worst suspicions proved to be true. Only a small band of warriors were in the camp, mostly wounded from the Fetterman fight. These men stumbled to their feet in an attempt to protect the camp while the soldiers cut them down with sabers and pistols.

Even though outnumbered, the warriors fought bravely, and no sadness filled my heart as they died. Men died in war. That was the nature of things. But when I beheld the women, old people, little children running from the crazed soldiers, I couldn't stand it.

I ran forward as I saw a boy not yet half grown run from a lodge as his mother warded off a soldier. The soldier ran his saber through the woman, lifting her from the ground. Then the same soldier started after the boy.

My legs were as strong as ever, but my heart was weak. I neared the boy, but the soldier reached him first. The man, a corporal, swung his saber at the boy, cutting off an ear. Then the corporal slashed the boy's right arm off. When I reached the bloody child, the corporal grinned. Then the saber flashed a third time, and the life I had sought to save was gone. Only the smell of death lingered.

"Sorry, boy," the corporal said. "You got to catch your own injuns. I got this one."

I walked away as the corporal began mutilating the corpse.

"Animals, dogs," I whispered to the wind. "All things are within all men. I pray I'll never grow fond of killing."

Walking into the Sioux camp, my head grew light. My stomach rumbled as I watched the soldiers ripping the limbs from children and cutting open women. The few warriors to be found were mutilated so that one who happened upon their bodies would not have known that they were human.

Trinkets, scalps, even skin and fingers were taken. It was a nightmare of unrestricted viciousness. I became sick, spilling my stomach on the buffalo grass. Then I made my way back to the supply wagons.

As I walked, a Sioux warrior, badly wounded and bleeding from his shoulder, bounded from the trees into my path. He had a look of terror in his eyes, and I reached for my pistol. He waved a war lance in his right hand, probing toward my stomach. He pierced the flesh of my left forearm, but as I winced with pain, I shot him twice in the chest. The Sioux fell to his knees, chanting the words which called his death. Then he fell on his face.

I stood over the man for many minutes. Soldiers rode past me as I stood with the smoking pistol in my hand. Some yelled words of praise. Others slapped me on the shoulder. But I was sick inside with the knowledge that I'd killed a man, stricken from life a fellow creature.

I'd come to the camp to save a small boy, and I'd ended up killing a man. Now I was one of the soldiers. My side of the battle had been chosen for me.

Then I saw something move in the trees. At first I thought it was just my horror flashing illusions before my eyes. But a second movement convinced me. I walked into the woods, every instinct accumulated over the years springing into life. The pain which burned through my arm awakened the will to survive in me, and I swung my pistol in front of me.

The cries of the dying filled the air, but I had ears only for the crack of branches up ahead of me. Then I walked into a clearing and found what I sought.

There were six of them. A near naked warrior in the center was surrounded by five small children. Something inside me warned me to fire, but the humanity that was inside my heart, that had never left me, bid me to put aside my gun.

"I come in peace," I told them in the tongue of the Sioux. "I will not bring your deaths."

The frightened children huddled closer to the warrior than before.

"It is over," I said. "I know the Sioux. The soldiers are busy in the camp. No one will bring your death this day."

"Will you not bring my death?" the warrior asked, hiding his head from me.

"I have no heart for killing Sioux," I told him. "I have hunted with the Sioux, have ridden with the Sioux, have shared the secrets of my heart with the Sioux."

"Then why have you come, Cougar Claw?" the voice asked.

"I am Cougar Claw," I said. "But I do not know you."

"I am no one to know," the warrior said. "I am as dead as if my scalp rested on the lodge pole of the Crow. I chant my last words soon. But you know Antelope Foot, who is behind me."

"Antelope Foot?" I asked. "Are you there, my brother?"

Antelope Foot stepped from behind the others, his head bandaged so that only one eye was not covered.

"Cougar Claw, why have you come into my lands?" he asked me. "Why do you raise your hand in anger against the Sioux?"

"I ride with my people even as you ride with yours," I told him. "I have ridden the country these many weeks, but I have taken no life before this day."

"Yes, I read that much in your eyes," he said. "But how can you call me brother when there is blood of my people upon your hands?"

"And you?" I asked. "Have you not killed the soldiers? Were you not there when Captain Fetterman and his men were killed?"

"I kill many long knife," he said weakly. "But they ride against my people. I do not ride out upon the white man's villages to shoot down his children."

"I don't hunt children," I told him. "I walked into the camp to save the children, but my legs do not carry me as swiftly as they once did. I have saved no one, not even myself. My heart is heavy with the death of too many innocents."

"Would you have us believe you will not shoot these children?" the other warrior asked. "Antelope Foot and I would hand over our lives if you would spare the children."

"I come to take no man's life," I said. "They must go quickly, though, for the soldiers may search these woods."

"Go, little ones," Antelope Foot told them. "Be as the wind. Red Cloud, our father, will come for you."

The children scrambled away. Then the nameless warrior stood up and chanted. In a moment, the old man fell, his eyes covered by death.

"Well, Cougar Claw," Antelope Foot said to me, "it has come to this. I am weak with fever, but I wait for my death as a Sioux. I stand ready for my death."

"You must seek it elsewhere," I told him. "I cannot take your life."

"The white man has killed my father, my brothers, my sisters. All that I know burns in the camp you have come from. My spirit walks the world alone now. My life has been taken already."

"Would you kill me, Antelope Foot?" I asked him, putting my pistol in my belt. "Would you put your knife through my heart, shutting my eyes forever? Would you carry my scalp on your belt?"

"Why do you come here, Cougar Claw?" he asked. "You do not walk the valleys in search of death. You do not come here to close the eyes of the Sioux. You are still my brother, even as when we shared the night of the cougar upon the distant mountain. My brother, do you not remember the thunder I spoke of so many nights ago? It has lit the skies for many moons. Would you save my life this night only to take it tomorrow?"

"No," I said, frowning. "I do not ride here in search of the Sioux. I don't want these hunting grounds. I don't seek to build a white man's road into Montana for the men who seek the yellow powder. I would have these places remain as they were."

I brushed aside the tears that were clouding my eyes.

"I believe in the things we spoke of that night before I killed the cougar and came to be a man," I said. "I believe in honor and courage and truth."

"This will always be," he said to me. "As long as you walk, there will be truth in your heart, Cougar Claw. Never lose that part of you which is from the mountain. That part of you which you seek here, the part of you which comes from the long knife, you must put aside as you would a moccasin which has walked too many summers."

"That was why I came," I said. "To try to belong to the world of my people. But I have no people. I am a man lost in the pass between the mountain and the valley."

"You will find your peace," he told me. "There is always a place for honor. You would take this from me this day," he said, using his healthy left arm to remove a small silver necklace from his neck.

"This belong to Painted Bow," he said. "It come from old people who live many summer ago in mountains past great buffalo valleys. My father given this by his father."

"I can't take it," I said.

"I give this to you, my brother," he said. "You will wear this as long as we are brothers. It will send my spirit flying to you when you are in need of strength. I do not know if I will see you again, Cougar Claw. It is all I can leave you with."

"Here I stand, the trader, with nothing to give you in return," I sighed.

"You have given the greatest of things, Cougar Claw," he said. "You have given my life to me."

"But it was a debt I owed," I told him. "You gave my life to me when the cougar struck me down."

"Ah, but you saved me from that cougar," he said, smiling. "I wear even this day its claws. They keep the evil spirit from calling my death."

"I wear mine, too," I said. "Now I will wear this necklace, too."

"Ride with the spirits of the wind," he said to me.

"Be careful," I answered.

Then he walked softly into the woods and disappeared into the world beyond my eyes. I suspected that I would never again lay my eyes upon him in this life.

CHAPTER 16

I returned to the supply wagons to find the soldiers wild with victory. The Sioux village was burning, and no survivors could be seen. It was but a small village really, only a dozen or so lodges, but the victory had seemed to satisfy the thirst for revenge that filled the hearts of the soldiers.

As I bound my wounded left arm, I brooded over the deaths I'd seen. No more than twenty or thirty Sioux, mostly women and children, had been killed, though. I figured most of the people had escaped into the woods, but whether they would live through the coming winter without lodges or clothing remained a question.

I never again rode with the Army into the Powder River Valley. The peace commission was created, and Colonel Carrington was called back East. The soldiers in the little forts were reinforced, but the war settled down into a series of raids.

I spent the winter in Fort Laramie helping Trader Jim at the store. My eyes were clouded by all that I'd seen, and no one asked me about my experiences.

The war shifted like the wind. The white man's army that had thundered through the valley in the beginning now rode with fear. Red Cloud had shut down the road into Montana, and no man or beast reached safety beyond the northernmost fort. The Indians didn't know it, but with the coming of winter, the white man had lost his war for control of the Powder River Valley.

I came to be fifteen that winter, and at last I came to take on the look of a man. My voice deepened, and the first signs of a mustache appeared on my lip. I became taller, stronger, more confident. But a new sadness settled over me, and I found my spirit lost in the midst of the fort and the soldiers.

April of 1867 brought the peace commission, and soon word was sent to Red Cloud that the white man no longer wished to kill Sioux. No more men were to die over the road to Montana. The great white father had decided the Sioux could keep their hunting grounds.

The Sioux began to gather in their numbers outside the fort, and it was like the old times again. Trader Jim and I went to the camps, trading for hides and beadwork. But there were less Sioux in the camps, and many of the children who should have run through the fires had been buried in the mountains during the winter.

For many days I walked through the camps of the Cheyenne and Sioux seeking Antelope Foot. I also asked for word of White Panther and Black Kettle. None of them were to be found. White Panther and Black Kettle were south of the Arkansas River where they'd agreed by treaty to camp. Antelope Foot was not spoken of.

I feared in my heart that he had fallen in battle. It would have been like him to take the greatest risk. But he finally rode into the Sioux camp the day before the treaty signing, and word came to me at the store.

"I have joy in my heart to see my brother strong and well," Antelope Foot said to me as I walked inside his new lodge. "You have grown tall this winter."

"Not so tall as you," I said. "You have healed well."

"As you have, my brother," he said, pointing to the scar I bore from the Sioux war lance.

"It was a clean wound," I told him. "I wouldn't have an arm if you'd struck me."

"He who struck you walks no more," Antelope Foot said. "It is said by many that a man who is marked by the dead cougar can only be killed by the spirits, Cougar Claw."

"Many things are sung around campfires which are made up in the minds of old women," I said. "I would rather trust

in a sharp knife and a keen eye than in a legend sung by warriors, even Sioux warriors."

My last remark pleased him, and he smiled.

"This you have said with great wisdom, my brother. Tell me this, have you heard of the peace talk? Is this good talk?"

"Talk of peace is always good," I told him.

"Yes," he said. "But is this peace one we will not fight for again tomorrow? Does this mean you will ride no more into the valley of my fathers?"

"I will ride no more there unless it is in search of my brother," I told him. "Those lands are yours, and should stay so. I believe the man who comes from Washington speaks with the true spirit. He wishes only peace. Too many have died in this land of ours. We will speak no more of dying for many moons."

"Many moons?" he asked. "How many moons? Will our sons, Cougar Claw, know that we are brothers, or will they ride against each other in the buffalo valleys? Will I come to call your death?"

"If you do, you will have it," I said. "I'll never come to call your death."

"I know this to be true this day," he said, "but it will not always be so. Today the Sioux are as the mountain. The mountain has not moved. But the white man is still the river, and the river sweeps all before it away."

"Maybe this time the river will seek another valley," I said. "The great white father does not like to see his soldiers die in so great a number."

"I pray this is so," he said. "But I do not call you to speak of dying. We dance this night. Do you still run with the wind, my brother?"

"I run with the clouds," I said. "I am here, then gone. Would you run with me?"

"As we once did," he said, laughing. "You were too great of heart for me that day. But your heart is heavy this night. I fear I will run from you like a deer."

We raced twice that night, and I surprised myself with the

new power inside me. Only a few months before my feet had seemed weighted with lead. Now they had regained their old nimbleness, and they didn't betray me once. I flew across the soft earth like the eagle crosses the sky, and Antelope Foot couldn't catch me. I won both races.

As we ate beside his fire, we spoke of the old ways, the old times. We told stories of Painted Bow and Blanket Jim Bridger and the boy named Cougar Claw. I remembered that boy with fondness in the way a man always remembers what he was before he came to be himself.

"The boy is the sapling which grows into the tree," Antelope Foot said. "Those as you and I grow into mighty pines, strong and tall on the mountain. Those who are weak are broken apart for firewood or eaten by horses."

"Yes," I said. "Those who are strong enough to hear the angry thunder and live on to hear the summer rains again will always be part of the mountain."

"You should have been born a Sioux," Antelope Foot told me. "You have too much heart for a white man."

"I am more Sioux than white man," I said, pointing to the necklaces I wore around my neck. "I remember always my brother, Antelope Foot, and his people."

"And your brother thinks of you, Cougar Claw," he told me. "Your brother feels naked riding after buffalo with you not at his side. Would you come to hunt with me this summer? Would you come to live beside me in the buffalo valleys?"

"I would like to do that," I said.

The next day when the treaties were signed, there was much celebrating. Antelope Foot and I feasted on a pig I'd traded for at the fort. We sat and watched the stars from the porch of the store, feeling tall and proud and full of our manhood.

"The soldiers have been defeated by Red Cloud," I said.

"Yes," Antelope Foot said. "This is the first time the white man has come to write the peace as we say it. But it will not last."

"Why not?" I asked. "The white man is more interested in Oregon and California than in Wyoming. There is said to be gold around the South Pass, but that lies beyond the lands of the Sioux."

"We have burned the white man's forts in the land of our fathers," Antelope Foot said. "But this is not the end of the white man. He will not forget the Sioux. He is too much like the grizzly bear."

"The grizzly bear?" I asked.

"Yes, my brother," he told me. "Have you not heard of the grizzly bear who once ate the leg of a sheep? It is said the sheep gave his leg to the grizzly bear so as to save the rest of him. The grizzly bear was not to be trusted, though. The bear ate the leg, but he thought to himself, why should he be content to eat the leg of the sheep when he could eat the whole sheep? The sheep could not run with three legs like the bear could run with four, so the bear ate the poor sheep."

"The white man is like the grizzly bear," I said. "But the sheep did not make the grizzly bear sick to his stomach when the grizzly ate the leg. The grizzly bear would not have come again to taste the sheep that had filled his belly with sickness."

"You have much of the white man inside you, Cougar Claw," Antelope Foot said to me. "You twist the stories I tell to fit your purpose. This the treaty makers do."

"It is the heart of a man who would see no more death," I said. "I have seen too many bodies resting in the buffalo grass. I would not lie there myself."

"You will never lie there," he told me. "I will not lie there. We are of the mountain. We will sing our death chant on the mountain."

"That may be," I said. "Many moons will come before that," I said. "Many moons."

"Do you see the stars that fall from the sky?" he asked me.

"I see them," I said, watching three shooting stars blaze across the heavens.

"Our death will be like that," he said. "There will be the

death of a great brightness, a great courage, when the spirits call for us."

"Yes," I sighed. "The death of a great brightness."

As the night closed in around us, we shared that thought.

CHAPTER 17

I passed two more summers on the plains with Antelope Foot. They were times of great adventures. We hunted buffalo and elk, fished the rivers and streams.

In 1868 I turned seventeen. I stood close to six feet tall, and I was as strong and as swift as any young Sioux warrior. The years had passed in a gentle fashion, leaving my spirit strong and full of confidence.

There were many young men among the Oglala Sioux who never understood Antelope Foot's friendship with a white man. There were many at the fort who couldn't understand how I could go off each summer to live with the Sioux. But we didn't concern ourselves about them.

My mother kept to herself most of the time now. Trader Jim still operated his store, but he no longer rode out in his wagon to trade with the tribes. I still kept his accounts, but more and more he now traded for the silver coins he had once detested.

My mother planned a formal celebration of my birthday, co-hosting a party at the post commander's home. The young ladies of the fort were invited, and the officers brought their wives. It was to be a night of dancing and idle chatter as befit the polite society of Philadelphia or Baltimore.

I hated the party. I knew few of the young ladies of the fort, and I had nothing in common with the officers. We lived in different worlds, and I was less than anxious to find myself accepted by the other one.

My friends were not there. None of my Sioux companions would be allowed near the post commander's house, and my other friends on the post were mainly small merchants and enlisted men. Neither group was included in Mother's list of acceptable persons.

When I left early following three dances with the colonel's daughter, Mother was furious.

"I arranged this entire party for you, Johnny," she told me. "I simply cannot understand how you could turn your back on all those people."

"Those people were more relieved that I left than I was," I told her. "They don't like me or my ideas."

"Johnny, you don't know that," she said. "The colonel has a great fondness for you. His brother is a senator, you know."

"What difference does that make?" I asked. "Senators belong in another world. I don't need senators to ride the plains and climb the mountains."

"Come with me," she told me, leading me by the hand. "I have something to show you."

We walked the short distance to the little house behind the store. Then she took me into her room and opened a small black chest.

"There are many things in this chest, Johnny," she said. "Among them is a bank book. Whenever your grandfather put some money aside, I mailed it to a banker friend in Philadelphia. The account is in your name, Johnny."

"It might as well be in France," I said. "I don't need money."

"You will when you get back East," she said. "There will be so many expenses. Clothes, lodging, tuition."

"What are you talking about?" I asked. "I don't intend to go away from here."

"Johnny, there's something else in here. Something you should read. It's a letter from your father," she said.

I froze for a minute.

"What? You mean Father left a letter I've never seen?"

"He left it with me to read to you when you were old enough to understand," Mother explained.

"But I've been old enough for a long time," I complained.

"Listen," she said. "I'll read the part of it that's for you.

'And so, dearest, you'll have to talk to John. Tell him I've always been proud of him and always will be. He's a good boy with a strong heart and a firm will. He'll make a place for himself in this world. I know it won't be easy for you to bring up Johnny all alone, but I want him to grow up to be somebody. All my life I've been around forts and soldiers. I want Johnny to grow up to be something different. I'd like him to do good for people, be a doctor maybe. My mother has the money to ensure his entrance to any school he chooses. All you have to do is get him prepared for college.'"

"I don't understand," I said. "If Father felt like that, why did we leave Pennsylvania?"

"Because you weren't ready for the East then. You would never have been strong enough to be a Whitlock. Your grandmother would have smothered you. You had to go East as a man."

"Mother, I won't go," I said. "Father had his dream, and I have mine. This is my home, and this is the place I'll die."

"Johnny, you can't spend your whole life hunting buffalo and telling stories around a campfire."

"Mother, you know the West. You were born here. Please don't keep pushing me into a world where I don't belong. I'd do anything for you, but I just can't leave the only place where I've ever belonged."

She argued and argued, but I felt in my heart that I belonged where I was.

That soon changed. Sad news came from the South. I heard some soldiers talking to Trader Jim. My grandfather turned white as a sheet, then walked back to where I was standing.

"Johnny, come back here with me," he said.

"Yes, sir," I answered, following him to the storeroom.

"Son, do you still have that old Cheyenne knife?" he asked.

"You know I do," I said. "I always keep it with me. It's the one Black Kettle gave to me."

"I've got some bad news for you, Johnny. Black Kettle is dead."

"Dead?" I asked. "He wasn't all that old."

"No, son," he said. "But he was a Cheyenne, and that was fatal."

"I don't think I understand."

"The Army fought a battle on the Washita River," he told me. "The Washita is inside lands protected by treaty, but the 7th Cavalry under General Custer rode down Black Kettle and wiped out the best part of the southern Cheyenne."

"You don't mean rode down," I said. "You mean murdered."

"It means the same thing," he told me. "Black Kettle saw it coming after Sand Creek."

"Sand Creek?" I asked.

"There was a massacre of the Cheyenne by a bunch of Colorado militiamen at Sand Creek. It pretty well ended the Cheyenne. They say Black Kettle stood there waving a big American flag. They just fired anyway."

"Won't there ever be trust between the Indians and the white men?" I asked.

"I don't suppose so," he said, frowning. "At any rate, it may be that this is a good year to die."

"Who else is dying?" I asked.

"Our way of life, son," he said. "I've been thinking about starting a horse ranch. I need some good great-grandsons to keep it going."

"Where would we start such a ranch?" I asked.

"Well, it'd be a few years away. We'd need a partner with a good education."

"You've been talking with Mother," I said.

"Johnny, she's after your own best interests. I think you should go back East and try to make a place for yourself. I don't think you'd enjoy being around when the Sioux meet their end."

"The Sioux?" I asked.

"The Sioux and the Cheyenne are the last of the great tribes of the plains. The Cheyenne are finished. The Sioux are bound to be next."

"But the treaty," I objected.

"You know what treaties mean to generals," he told me. "And we have a general for a president."

By the end of the week I told Mother that I would go East. She made the arrangements, and I prepared to say my good-bys.

I walked sadly around the fort, telling the soldiers and shopkeepers I knew so well that I would soon be swallowed up by that other world beyond the great waters. Most of the soldiers were envious. They couldn't understand my reluctance to leave the harsh Laramie winter for the world of Philadelphia parlors and ballrooms.

With my good-bys completed at the fort, I saddled a horse, pulled a new coat made from buffalo hides over my shoulders, and set out for the Powder River.

It was never easy to journey in the winter, but I could never have gone without seeing Antelope Foot, without trying to explain what was pulling me away from the world we both loved more than life itself.

I reached the village on the fifth day of my journey. The snows had been heavy, and the wind had chilled me through even the heavy buffalo hide. But as I rode into the Sioux camp, I was warmed by the fresh smile upon the face of my friend.

"I welcome my brother, Cougar Claw, to the camp of my people," he told me, helping my half-frozen body down from my horse.

"I come with a heavy heart, Antelope Foot," I said. "I go away soon."

"Away?" he asked, a puzzled look upon his face. "To what place?"

"Across the great waters," I told him. "I go back to the place I came from."

"Why is this?" he asked me. "You do not belong to the other world. This is not right."

"No, it is not right," I said, frowning. "But it is what must be."

"You are wrong, Cougar Claw," he told me. "You will go

beyond the waters and find yourself much changed. You will fall under the magic of the yellow powder. You will be like the others. It would be your death truly as much as if my lance lay buried in your heart."

"Haven't you heard of the Washita?" I asked. "Black Kettle is dead. White Panther is dead. The Cheyenne people are no more. You told me of the angry thunder. I feel it coming, my brother. I would not stand here and watch all that I love die before my eyes."

"Then come with me, my brother. Hunt with me, ride with me, fight at my side. This is as it should be."

"For how long?" I asked him. "How many moons would find us happy? How long would the long knife soldiers let us hunt and fish and grow? If I stayed, our deaths would be written in the mountains. To live is a great thing, my brother."

"To leave the mountains is not to live, Cougar Claw. To live for even five summers more upon the buffalo valleys would be enough. To die with my lance in my hand upon the tall mountain is enough for me. It would be a death that men would sing of."

"It's right for you," I said. "But I have my mother, my father's dreams to think of. If I was alone, I would ride with you until my days ended on the mountain. But I must be my father's son this day, even as you are your father's."

"This I understand," he said. "But I mourn your death, my brother. You will come no more to the mountain. I will see you no longer."

"This bears heavy on my heart," I said. "I will miss our days of hunting and fishing. I will never be as warm in the other world as I have been sitting beside you around the council fire."

"You will stay with me this night?" he asked.

"Yes, but I must go soon. My mother waits."

"Come and meet my wife," he said, leading the way to his lodge.

She was a small woman for a Sioux. Her name was Tree Woman, and her face was simple and kind. I knew the first time I saw her that she was the wife of a chief. She was patient, understanding, strong enough to stand up to the long treks.

I noticed something else about her. A child was on the way. It was written on Antelope Foot's face, too, and I smiled at the thought.

"Your son will be born in the spring, my brother," I said. "You will have another companion on your hunts."

"But this will be many summers to come," he said. "Will you not stay until then?"

"I would if it was only my heart that I must listen to. But there are others to think of, and I have to follow the path I have set out on."

"Then it is settled. We will speak of this no more. Let us eat and be happy, thinking of other days."

"Yes," I said. "Other days."

I started back to Laramie the next morning with a heavy heart. I made the return trip in four days, for there was only the riding to be done. I stopped for nothing else.

I didn't see in the mountains or the river anything I wanted to remember better than I would already. Every mile of the snow-laden landscape was a part of me.

My final good-by was saved for Trader Jim. As Mother and I prepared to step into the wagon we would ride to the railroad, I turned to look at him. His face was older, and his shoulders sagged in a way they never had before. I looked into his eyes and read for the first time the coming of his death.

"Trader Jim, you have taught me so much. I wish I could pay you back in some small way for all you have shown me."

"Wasn't so much," he said. "Was all my pleasure."

"I'll miss you," I told him, reaching my arm around his tired old body.

"That's enough of this," he said, pushing me away. "You be on your way, Johnny Cougar Claw. This day it's time for you to be a man."

"Good-by," I said to him, shaking a tear from my eye.

As I looked a last, a final time upon his face, his eyes were bright and solemn. There was a sadness inside him that was matched in my heart. When we rode away, I knew I would never see him again in this life.

CHAPTER 18

Mother told me I would learn the ways of my people in the East. I had known from the first, though, that there was nothing I could be taught by the tall buildings and busy streets of the cities that I couldn't learn better from the mountains and streams I was leaving behind.

When we reached York, I took out my mother's great black traveling trunk and began packing away my prized possessions. I put my cougar claw necklace, my great buffalo hide cloak, my moccasins and rifle, even the silver necklace Antelope Foot had given me, inside the trunk. Closing the lid, I began my new life in the civilized world.

Grandmother Whitlock took a firm hand in my education, instructing me in table manners and polite chatter. In the fall, she sent me to Princeton University.

I studied hard, devoting myself to books on banking and business. I left the university four years later with a degree in finance, bound for Baltimore and a job in the bank of a Mr. Henry Bremmer.

Baltimore was a pleasant change for me. I never belonged at Princeton. The parties and small talk tested my patience, and even those I called friends knew I was different. They laughed at my stories about the West, but behind my back they made up stories and told jokes about me.

That first summer in Baltimore was full of wonder. My work was challenging, and at a small party on the Fourth of July Mr. Bremmer introduced me to his niece, Miss Anna Kielgaard.

Anna was like no one I'd ever met. She was soft and sensitive, and there was a beauty to her that radiated. I never wanted to be apart from her, and we were married that September.

Our first three years together were wonderful. Anna brought me a daughter, Emily, and we purchased a house in the country. We lived quietly, enjoying the rolling Maryland countryside. But it was an unreal world, and it didn't last.

The first shadow which fell across our lives was the death of my mother. We buried her beside my father in the family plot in York, and Emily and I cried together. Anna was immune to tears, but she seemed powerless to drive away the gloom which smothered me.

Worse news followed. The West of my youth was torn apart by the war which Antelope Foot had warned me of. Custer, the general who had brought death to Black Kettle and the Cheyenne, had ridden to his own death on the banks of the Little Bighorn River.

The Baltimore newspapers called it a massacre. The people cried out for revenge. Every day brought news that bore heavily on my soul. New armies of blue-coated soldiers rode through the sacred lands of the Sioux, and one by one the great chiefs laid down their arms.

In all the years I'd been East I'd never really ceased to care what happened to the world of my youth, the world I would always love best. But Anna was with child again, and I didn't speak of it to her or anyone else.

Anna noticed, though. I didn't seem to care about things anymore. Even little Emily couldn't bring a smile to my face. I was distracted at the bank, and I couldn't concentrate. Even the birth of my first son, John Anderson Whitlock III, didn't change things.

Following the christening, Anna finally spoke to me about it.

"You want to go back," she said simply. "I've seen it on your face before, Johnny, but never like this. You're going this time."

"No," I told her sadly. "I can never go back. I don't think

there's anything there for me. Besides, I couldn't leave you and Emily and little Johnny."

"Are you really sure about that?" she asked me.

"I'm not sure about anything anymore," I said, taking her hand and leading her out into the garden. "But I'm sure that I need you."

Even the nights I spent holding the baby couldn't break the spell I was under, though. I awoke in the night from terrible nightmares. I saw Antelope Foot die a hundred times. And each time my heart died with him.

Each day I rose, dressed, kissed Anna, Emily, and John, and went to work. Each evening I returned, read the newspaper, ate dinner, and went to bed. But there was no laughter, no joy in the house. I was a man lost to the world.

Then one day a telegram arrived at the bank. The message was simple, briefly but thoughtfully worded. "Grandfather Jim Howard died July 20. Buried at Laramie. House and store await disposal. God bless you. E. Harrington."

"Old Mrs. Harrington," I whispered to the silence which filled my office. "I never would have known."

I thought back to the hundred different times Trader Jim had spoken about living too long.

"At least you won't have to know a time without the Sioux," I said softly. "You wouldn't have liked the world that's coming. You were too good for it."

A single tear wove its way across my cheek. Then it trickled down my chin and fell to my chest.

"You would not want tears from me," I said. "You taught me to stand tall against a clear sky. I will do that always."

After that, I became a man apart from people. We went nowhere, and my eyes never looked up at life. One night I went into the attic alone and opened the ancient trunk in which I'd placed the treasured relics of my past. As I took the painted knife Black Kettle had handed me a lifetime ago, I heard footsteps on the stairs below.

"Johnny?" Anna called to me. "Is that you?"

"Yes," I said, setting the knife down.

"What are you doing?" she asked me, walking to where I was standing. "What is all this?"

"I've never shown you this," I told her. "It's time now you saw everything."

First I showed her the knife. Then I showed her the necklace of cougar claws. I tenderly fingered moccasins I'd worn across prairie grasses. I showed her buffalo hide coats and buckskin trousers I'd outgrown long ago. There were also pictures of my parents, old schoolbooks, leather pouches, and Indian beadwork.

"You're very proud of all this, aren't you?" Anna asked me.

"I never thought about it that way," I said. "It's what I am."

"I never heard you say that before," she told me. "You usually say it's what you were."

"That's what I meant."

"No, it's not," she said. "It's what you'll always be. Johnny, don't tell me differently. I know you. I know you better than you know yourself. I love you more than anything else in this world, but it's you I love, not what you've become lately."

"What are you talking about?" I asked.

"You, Johnny. You don't belong here. You never will. Baltimore and Philadelphia might as well be China. I haven't seen you laugh or smile in days, not since you heard about your grandfather."

"He taught me about life," I said. "He helped me become everything that was ever important to me. And when I had to leave, he understood even that. I knew when I looked in his eyes the last time that I'd never see him again."

"You should have gone back when your mother died," she told me.

"I could never have gone back then," I said. "It would have been breaking a promise to Father and to her."

"You were old enough to do what you needed to do for yourself, Johnny. Now it's going to be hard. But you should go and do it anyway."

"Do what?" I asked.

"Go back to Fort Laramie," she said. "Go back to the mountains and the rivers. Find yourself."

"And you?"

"We'll be all right, Johnny. When you find a place where you can belong, we'll join you."

"The children won't belong out there," I said. "It's not a place for children."

"It was a place for you," she said. "You were happy there. You could teach little Johnny things you could never teach him here. I want you, Johnny. I need you. But I need the you you've kept buried these last few weeks, not the one I see now."

"Is that really what you want?" I asked.

"Yes," she said. "Go back and make peace with your past. Then come back or stay. It won't matter as long as it's your choice. I can go anywhere, and so can the children. All we want is a home with you."

"But there's so much that could happen," I told her.

"That's true of any place," she said. "But you can't spend your life worrying about that. Your father didn't. We need you, me and Emily and little Johnny. But we want the man who killed a cougar when he was still a boy, not that shell of a man that's been here lately. If you can find a place out there where you belong, we'll come. I can be a very tough woman when I need to be. And if you find that the place that has room for you has no room for us, then we'll find a way to go on without you."

She said those final words with tears in her eyes. I reached over and took her in my arms. We held each other in the way we had our first night together.

When the house outside Baltimore had been sold, I took Anna and the children to York to stay with my grandmother. Then I boarded the train headed West. I felt like I was going home.

CHAPTER 19

The West I returned to was a different place from the one I'd left behind. There was a railroad cutting across the great plains to the south, and small farms lined the Platte. On my first trip to Fort Laramie we'd crossed hundreds of miles without seeing so much as a stray deer. Now there were people everywhere.

But it was not the people or the railroads or the farms which unsettled me. It was something unseen, something which belonged in the panorama of my western world. Absent from sight were the great herds of buffalo, the brightly painted tepees of the Cheyenne and Arapaho villages.

The absence of the tribes brought back to me the terrible reality of the world in which I lived. The days of proud warriors and adventurous traders had died with old John Crandell in the Powder River Valley ten years before. The world I now looked upon was filled with greed and hatred. I neither understood nor found affection for that world.

I rode the proud sorrel I'd bought in Omaha onto a rise of ground overlooking the Platte near the fort. The river there had always been like an old friend, but even it seemed to have changed.

When I rode into the fort, I hardly recognized the place. All kinds of new little shops and houses had sprung up where the Sioux had once camped. A small city had appeared from out of the buffalo grass of the prairie. Little children now ran through what had become small streets. I looked past them at the soldiers who patrolled the entrance to the post.

One place had changed little. The old store retained its bat-

tered walls and dusty windows. As I rode past it, I fought
back a sigh from deep within me. The thought of the store
without Trader Jim was more than I could bear. I slid down
from the saddle and led the sorrel into the stable. After the
horse was fed, watered, and rubbed down, I walked over to
the house.

Mrs. Harrington had tended to things in my absence. The
linens were stored in their places, and the furniture was as
free from dust as it had been when Mother lived in the little
room down the hall.

Everywhere I looked there were reminders of what had
been there before. I saw old schoolbooks that Trader Jim
couldn't have had use for. I saw old moccasins and vests that I
had worn in my childhood.

It surprised me that my grandfather had not traded those
little reminders of me to some other boy around the fort. But
there was a side to him that he kept hidden from me that
needed my ears for his stories, my eyes for his demonstrations
of leatherwork or riflery.

I walked through the house room by room in search of
someone who wasn't there. I felt the soft leathery touch of his
deerskin coat, smelled the tobacco scent of his pipe. I even
handled his rifles and knives. But though I seemed to touch
his spirit, I didn't feel his rough hand on my shoulder as I
once had, the way I needed so desperately on that September
afternoon.

I needed the words he would have spoken to explain what
had happened to me. I needed his help to search out the me
I'd left behind. But he wasn't there, and I left the house
behind me.

The store was but a shadow of what it had been. There
were few barrels of flour or boxes of cartridges on the shelves.
The stacks of buffalo hides and deerskins which once crowded
the storeroom where I slept were gone. Looking through the
ledgers, I saw what I'd expected. Trader Jim had converted
his trading stock into cash. There was almost a thousand dollars in the post bank.

"You knew it, you old trader," I whispered to the chair he would have been sitting in. "You saw the heavens. You read your death, and you knew I would come. You left the silver I would need in the other world, but I needed your words, your direction, not your money."

Mrs. Harrington found me that night sitting in that same chair.

"Johnny Whitlock," she said to me, "I brought you a bite of hot supper. Would you take it here or in the house?"

"Here's fine," I told her. "The house is too big and lonely for me."

"Well, I'll just put it on this little accounting table," she said, setting a small pot down there. "I'll make a little extra while you're here. I did that for your grandfather. He was a friend to us when we needed one."

"And you were a friend to him when he had no one else," I said.

"Tell me about yourself, John," she said, sitting down across from me.

"Not too much to tell. I've been in the East. I worked in a big bank in Baltimore. I have a wife and two small children."

"And you came back here?" she asked. "For the money?"

"No, ma'am," I said. "Money never much mattered to Trader Jim or me. I guess it was something else."

"He knew you'd come," she said, smiling in a distant way. "I never did understand that man, but he knew things. He could tell when the snows would come. He knew when a child would be born and when an old man's time had come."

"He learned it on the mountain," I said. "It's a spirit thing. He could read the skies. He could read a man's face, and he could look right through a man into his heart."

"He missed you when you left," she said. "I thought it was your mother at first, but it was you. He used to tell the story about you and Antelope Foot's race. He used to tell the soldiers about the cougar you killed. He was powerful proud of you, Johnny."

"He let me go," I said. "A single word from him would have kept me here."

"It wasn't to be, Johnny. He knew that. He could read the future in the skies. He knew that if you stayed here, you'd die with the old ways."

"And am I alive now?" I asked. "He sent me off to a world I could never belong to."

"Johnny, he knew that," she said. "He told me once that you would come back. When I asked when, he told me it would be in the autumn of his death."

"But why did I wait until he was gone?" I asked. "Why didn't I come earlier?"

"You know that," she told me. "You didn't come for the same reason he could never have called you back. The old ways were dead. To come back would have been to surrender to their death."

"I don't understand," I said.

"Yes, you do, Johnny. But what I don't understand is why you come now. Why do you come here when you got a wife and children back East? If you don't need the money, what do you need?"

"Myself," I told her. "Somehow I misplaced myself. I knew my heart when I was a boy here, but now I'm lost. I may not find the secrets to who I am here, but I know no other place to search for them."

"You're going back to the mountains then," she said.

"Are you surprised?" I asked.

"No," she said. "But it'll be dangerous. The Sioux that are out there are deadly. They've killed many white men. You won't hear tales of Antelope Foot and Cougar Claw on the winds now. All you'll hear is Sitting Bull and Crazy Horse, Gall and Low Dog."

"The war chiefs?"

"War is all the Sioux have left. War and death. You have more left to you."

"Do I?" I asked her.

"There's a man who would buy the store and the house.

This man would pay a pretty piece of change. Or you could keep the store and bring your family."

"I'll never be a trader," I said.

"You could be. You have the eye that's to be trusted."

"But not the heart for it," I told her.

"They have the railroad just to the south. They say men make new towns every day."

"They would need banks then," I said. "Maybe when I come back . . ."

"If you go, you might not come back," Mrs. Harrington warned.

"If I don't go, I won't be here at all," I said. "A man without his spirit is no man at all."

"Now you're sounding like your grandfather."

"And like myself," I said to her.

The next morning I walked around the fort, greeting old friends with smiles, sharing stories I'd told a thousand times before.

In the afternoon as I cleaned out the storeroom and packed away the last reminders of the boy I'd once been, I heard a knock on the door of the store. I walked to the door and opened it. In the doorway stood a young man with a look of freshness upon his face. He looked no older than twenty, but he had bright gold lieutenant's braid on his shoulders.

"Sir," the lieutenant said, saluting. "Colonel Masterson's compliments, sir. He awaits your pleasure and convenience, sir."

I hadn't heard the crisp words of a colonel's aide in many years. I'd often heard such talk as a little boy in my father's army camps. It brought a trace of a smile to my lips.

"Tell the colonel it will be my privilege to see him," I told the lieutenant.

"Would you accompany me now, sir?" he asked.

I put on my hat and walked with the lieutenant to the post commander's house. I'd danced there, attended parties with ladies and gentlemen in their polished buttons and bright lace dresses. All I saw now was an old white house that was in need of fresh paint.

The colonel was an old man. As was common, he'd held his rank since the war, trading the stars of a general for the more secure privileges of a colonel in the regular Army.

"Good to see you, Whitlock," the colonel said to me, extending his hand. "I served with your father."

"He was a good soldier," I said. "A brave man and a good father to me."

"He was the kind of man that makes a son proud," the colonel said. "I hear fine things of you, too, young man."

"The colonel is kind," I said.

"The colonel is only repeating what he's heard from others," he told me. "I heard you used to ride with the Sioux."

"No, sir," I said. "I used to hunt with them sometimes, but I never rode with the Sioux. I rode with Colonel Carrington into the Powder River Valley. I never fought the whites."

"That's not what I was meaning to say," the colonel told me. "I mean you know their ways. You know the land."

"As well as many," I said. "Better than most."

"Have you ever heard of a Sioux buck named Twisted Nose?"

"Twisted Nose?" I asked. "I walked the camps of the Oglala and Brule many years, but I never heard of such a man. Is he Sans Arc? I don't know him."

"He is Oglala Sioux," the colonel said. "It's said he got his name fighting Crook on the Rosebud. He isn't an old man. How long have you been away?"

"Almost ten years," I said. "If he was a very young man, I wouldn't know him."

"How much do you know of the situation here?" he asked.

"Only what I've read. The Sioux wiped out Custer. Since then General Crook and General Terry have been hunting them down."

"Most of the Sioux are gone," he said. "Sitting Bull took a bunch of them into Canada. They don't worry me. The ones that worry me are with Twisted Nose up in the Powder River country. They say Twisted Nose has sworn a blood oath to kill every white man that sets foot in the hunting grounds of the Sioux."

"And the Army rides after him?" I asked.

"That's our orders. Most of the patrols operate out of Fort Fetterman. We serve as a relay station for orders, supplies, and reinforcements."

"And the patrols burn their villages, shoot their women, ride down the children," I said, remembering. "But the warriors fight on."

"Yes, they fight on," he said. "Look, son, the Sioux are finished. Most of them have already turned themselves in. Red Cloud and the others never left the reservation. The people back East want the hide of every Sioux. You've been there. You can imagine what my orders are."

"Yes," I said, frowning.

"I don't want that, Whitlock. The only way to prevent that is to get these Sioux back to the reservation. I only know of one man who could do that. He's the man the Sioux know as Cougar Claw. They trust you."

"Cougar Claw was me in another lifetime," I said. "The Sioux you speak of would never trust a white man."

"I know only one thing about the Sioux," the colonel said. "They honor courage, and they can read it in a man's eyes. I don't have a man I could send to them who could talk them into coming in. But you they'd listen to."

"Why?" I asked. "Is this Twisted Nose such a fierce warrior that he defeats all you send against him?"

"It's not a matter of that," Colonel Masterson said. "Every day that Twisted Nose lives, the legends about him spread. Already there's talk that he's not a man. Some of my soldiers who've fought him say he isn't a man. They say they've shot him a dozen times, but he never bleeds. They say he's a ghost, appearing out of nowhere to kill. Then he vanishes."

"Do you believe this?" I asked.

"I believe soldiers who are frightened see things. A man can't ride through a bullet."

"And they say Twisted Nose is a ghost?"

"They say he's a devil," the colonel said. "The Oglala believe he's some kind of avenging angel. Some of the ones we've captured swear he's the man that killed Custer."

"There's a story behind every rock in the mountains," I said. "But if this Twisted Nose is making a stand, he will be a hard man to kill. The Sioux never bend once they prepare themselves for death."

"That brings me to you," he said. "We have supply wagons we need to get into Montana. Every time we get them rolling, this Indian band hits."

"I don't see what that has to do with me," I told him.

"I want you to lead a company of soldiers into the mountains. I want you to speak with Twisted Nose. Tell him we don't wish his death. Tell him to come in. If he does, he will live."

"I won't lie to him," I said. "I know it doesn't matter to the Army whether an Oglala Sioux warrior dies."

"Then tell him about the wagons," the colonel said. "Explain to him what you've seen in the East. Speak to him like you would to a brother."

"If he was my brother, I would fight at his side," I said, startling the colonel.

"You're not afraid of this man, are you?"

"How can I be?" I said. "I understand him. He would rather die than see the death of his world. A man should never outlive his time."

"You speak more like an Indian than a white banker from Baltimore," the colonel told me with a smile.

"I've been told something like that before, but not in a very long while."

"Then you'll go with my men?"

"I'll go, but you've got to promise me a chance to talk to Twisted Nose before you shoot up his camps."

"You have that promise," the colonel said.

"When do we start?" I asked him.

"You ride with Lieutenant Hastings tomorrow at daybreak. Does that meet with your approval?"

"Yes, sir," I told him.

"The lieutenant will wait for you at the gate," Colonel Masterson said, leading me out of the room. "I wish you the greatest luck at Fort Fetterman."

"Thank you, sir," I said, leaving the room.

Walking across the parade ground, I felt a new power in my legs. There was a purpose to my life I hadn't known in years.

I spent the rest of the day packing up clothes and guns that had once been mine or Trader Jim's. When I had everything in its proper place, I saw the man at the fort who wished to buy the store. I sold it to him, then carried the trunks of clothes and guns, books and trinkets to the army warehouse for safekeeping.

With my business attended to, I saw to the feeding of my horse. After a simple dinner of beef and beans, I fell into a shallow sleep on my last night in the little storeroom I had known as home.

My dreams were filled with Cougar Claw and Antelope Foot. I killed the cougar three times, and I lost count of the trout I took from the mountain streams to the north. But the ghostlike face of Twisted Nose rode across the world of my youth, and I woke in a shiver. The danger was not part of a boy's story. It was very close and very real.

CHAPTER 20

I rose long before dawn that next morning. The air was filled with a sudden chill, and I wrapped myself in a blanket. My bare feet tingled with the cold, and I rushed to get into a pair of buckskin trousers. Then I slipped my feet into a pair of boots covered with buffalo hair, and the warmth returned to my toes.

For a shirt, I chose one of coarse cotton. I also rolled two buckskin shirts into my blankets just in case the mountain proved to be cold. Then I slipped a buffalo hide vest over my shoulders and dragged an old bearskin coat along behind me.

I was almost dressed. From a small pouch I took the old necklace of silver Antelope Foot had left me in another lifetime. Then I added my cougar claws. Finally, I slipped the painted Cheyenne knife given me by Black Kettle into a scabbard on my left boot. Ready, I took a new Winchester under my arm and started for the stable.

After seeing to my horse, I took out a sheet of writing paper and sat down by myself. There was no light in the heavens, but I lit a candle and composed a short note to Anna. It was little enough to write, but if Twisted Nose proved the stronger, then I might never again have the opportunity.

Dearest Anna,

I am writing this letter from Laramie as I set out for the last time into the land of the Sioux. Even if I return to ride again, the Powder River Valley will never again belong to the Sioux.

I think I'll find myself here. There is a chill to the air, but my head is clear. I know there is only one road for me in this life, and my feet are on it. If I don't return, then know that at least I met my death as the boy who killed the cougar many years ago. If I return, then I will have found a place for all of us.

To John, my son, I can only say that his grandfather died young. But no matter how long a man lives, he is dead if he leaves his heart behind, lost in another place. My best wish for him would be that he grows into a man who can look others square in the eye any day of the year. Honor shouldn't be the first casualty of our new world.

For Emily I have no fears. She's as pretty as her mother, and I know she'll grow to have the grace and wit to match that beauty.

I have left with Colonel Masterson the accounts of my affairs in Maryland plus some monies Trader Jim left here for me. I hope you'll have the courage to come out West even if I'm not here.

You will always have my love, all of you. I am strong with the knowledge that I have yours. When we're together again, life will be as bright as a star on a clear evening.

> All my love,
>
> Johnny

With the letter written, I tucked it into the pocket of my vest and set out for my last stop. It was a quiet walk past the sentries and beyond the outbuildings of the fort. In the morning darkness, I felt very alone.

The little cemetery at Fort Laramie was surrounded by a simple iron gate. Inside were small wooden crosses and carved stone markers. On one side was the scaffold of a young Indian girl, the daughter of a chief. In the back was the fresh wooden cross that bore the name of Jim Howard.

I knelt down on one knee beside the grave and bowed my head.

"I'm sorry I waited so long to come," I said quietly. "You've been in my thoughts every day since I rode away from Laramie ten years ago. My heart was heavy when I read of your death, but I know it was the way it had to be."

I swallowed deeply and went on.

"Now I am about to set out with the Army into the land of the Sioux. There's a warrior named Twisted Nose who has it in his mind to kill every white man who enters the Powder River Valley. He would sing his death chant and the death chant of his people in the mountains that I love. If he dies with the lance in his hand, the old ways will die with him.

"Am I wrong to ride out with one last hope of saving part of what was? Am I wrong to want to find the boy who killed the cougar? Am I wrong to long for the sight of my brother, Antelope Foot? Why have I come back if it was not for these very reasons? And you always knew I would come."

I closed my eyes and saw his face appear as a vision in my mind. His eyes were bright, and I could almost sense his gentle touch on my shoulder.

"I left this place so long ago, but it is not the same place today that I leave behind. I ride off this morning to see if there is anything remaining for my heart to find. I know it is a fool who leaves behind what he loves to seek something that may not be there, but I would not have my spirit haunted by what I might have been."

I opened my eyes and stood up.

"I came here as a boy, and you taught me all there was that a man needed to know. Trader Jim, my grandfather and friend, may your spirit rest on the tallest mountain."

I added that last phrase with tears in my eyes. It was what Trader Jim had said at the burial of the old trapper, John Crandell. It was what my grandfather would have wanted to hear from the boy called Cougar Claw.

I walked away from the cemetery standing tall against a painted sky. The sun had broken the horizon, and the brilliant shades of orange and red that merged with the blue of the Wyoming sky brought a new warmth to me. I felt like I had my grandfather's blessing to ride into the mountains.

The rest of the dawn flew by. As Lieutenant Hastings organized the replacements for Fort Fetterman, I stopped by the colonel's office at the post headquarters and gave him my letter and the simple leather bag which contained the bank account books and details of the Maryland properties.

"If I don't come back, send these to my family," I told the colonel. "Don't mail them. Send them with an officer who's been reassigned."

"That won't be a problem," Colonel Masterson said. "But it appears to me you'd be a hard man to kill."

"A bullet kills a man very fast," I said, frowning. "Even a man of the mountains bleeds."

"Well, Whitlock, I wish you every good fortune," the colonel told me. "Twisted Nose is a difficult man to kill, too."

"We will speak to each other before either of us dies," I told him. "But if your soldiers intend to shoot Sioux, then many of them will not come back. If you make my words into lies, then I will be buried on the mountain, and the Sioux will never come in."

"I'm not lying to you," the colonel said. "My orders will be obeyed."

"Then maybe there's a chance for all of us," I said, leaving him with those words.

I joined Lieutenant Hastings on the parade ground. It only took a few minutes to saddle my horse and throw my blankets and spare clothing across my saddle. Then I joined the lieutenant at the head of the small column, and we rode out of Fort Laramie and onto the flat valley of the Platte.

I looked at the raw untested men that rode with us. They were very young or very old. They slumped in the saddle, and few of them looked like they belonged in an army. Some of them spoke with harsh accents, and some spoke only the roughest English.

I knew in two days we'd be in Fort Fetterman, camped in

the Powder River country where too many men had already died. If there was a fight, most of the men that rode behind me would ride no more. And I suddenly feared I might not ride again, either.

CHAPTER 21

Fort Fetterman was named in honor of the captain who had
led his men to their death in the Powder River country ten
years before. When Lieutenant Hastings and I led the replacements across the river into the fort, we were met by a
tall thin man in the uniform of an army captain.

Lieutenant Hastings saluted crisply, then handed the captain a dispatch case. The captain glanced over the orders,
then looked up at the lieutenant.

"Do any of these men have experience?" the captain asked.

"No, sir," the lieutenant answered.

"And you?"

"I served a year at West Point after graduation," Lieutenant Hastings said.

"A year at the Point?" the captain said, laughing. "A real
war hero I have here. Well, some of your men may be able to
shoot. Who's this in the buckskins, Kit Carson?"

"I'm John Whitlock," I said. "There should be something in
the orders about me."

"In the orders about you?" the captain said, breaking out in
a smile. "Are you the great pathfinder?"

"No, sir," I said. "I do know the mountains and the Sioux.
Colonel Masterson asked me to ride with those men into the
Powder River Valley to speak to Twisted Nose. The colonel
wants the Sioux to come in."

"The colonel wants them anywhere but where they are,"
the captain said. "Well, I'll need a man who knows the country when the time comes."

The captain's name was Henry B. Talbot, and I rode out of

the fort the next morning with a hundred men under his command. There were other expeditions fighting the Sioux and Cheyenne bands in the Bighorn Mountains or in the Missouri River Valley, but we were going after one man, the Sioux chief known as Twisted Nose.

We filed through the gate of the fort in a long column of twos. Captain Talbot led the column, but I found myself assigned a position in the rear with the supply wagons. I rode on my horse beside Lieutenant Hastings.

"Mr. Whitlock," the lieutenant said, "Captain Talbot must know what he's doing. He's been out here fighting the Indians for a long time."

"He thinks he knows what he's doing," I told the lieutenant. "But the mountains are a graveyard for men who think they know everything. Custer thought he knew the Sioux. A man who knew the Sioux would never ride into the mountains with his mind on war. The Sioux have been fighting since the beginning of time. Only our big guns, our numbers will win. If it was courage and strategy, the Sioux would be camping in Washington this minute."

"But they're only a bunch of Indians," Lieutenant Hastings said.

"Never forget that an Indian is a man," I said. "Never forget he feels pain. Never forget he hates you more than he fears death, and that to kill you is glorious for him."

We said nothing further as we crossed the Platte and headed into the Powder River Valley to the north. I stared at the yellow grass that swayed in the wind. There were no great buffalo herds in the valley now. And as I looked at the faint outline of the mountains in the distance, I knew that I wasn't riding to hunt elk with my brother, Antelope Foot. I was riding out in search of the Sioux. Worse, the men I rode with sang songs of death, and I found myself journeying to a land that might hold my grave.

On the third day we entered the heart of the valley. We camped that night beside the ruins of old forts Reno and Conner, which had been burned in the war ten years before.

The blackened logs scarred the beauty of the valley. I thought back to the faces I'd seen walking the walls of the forts. I remembered the galvanized Yankees who'd fought with courage and died of starvation or Sioux arrows. I remembered the Fetterman fight, the mutilated bodies that covered the prairie. But all that was in the past.

We rode deeper into the valley the next day. The captain had taken no Arikara scouts with him, and he kept me to the rear of the train. He'd traveled the Bozeman Trail many times, and he knew the way well. He rode in search of the Sioux, but he was blind to their signs.

I wasn't. I could see their pony tracks on the trails, and I could smell their fires on the wind. In the swaying of the buffalo grasses and the hooting of the owls I heard their voices. They were everywhere, and still we rode onward in a column of twos.

That night we camped on the banks of Crazy Woman Creek. A battle had been fought there in the summer of 1866. I found a rise of ground to lay my blankets on. I started to hack some limbs for a shelter when Lieutenant Hastings walked up.

"Mr. Whitlock, would you care to share my tent, sir?" he asked me.

"I'll make a shelter," I said. "The Army doesn't care too much for civilians sleeping in army tents. Besides, I'm kind of used to the stars."

"Sir, I don't have another officer in the command to sleep in there with me. I could do with a little company."

"Well," I said, looking into his youthful eyes, "I'm a rough sleeper. My wife claims I snore."

"Sir, you have an ear for the Sioux, though," the lieutenant said, shuffling his feet uncomfortably.

"You don't have to worry about an attack tonight," I said. "The captain says there aren't any Sioux."

"Sir, I can hear them," the lieutenant said. "I can feel something crawling up my back."

"There's hope for you then, lieutenant," I said, smiling.

"But the Sioux won't attack tonight. This camp is strong. The men are all grouped together, and the captain has guards out. Tomorrow morning the captain will string the command out on the road, and old Twisted Nose could chop this column up into little pieces."

"Will they attack?"

"They'll attack," I said. "They'll look into the eyes of Captain Talbot. Then they'll attack. Any Sioux can read the hatred in his eyes. They can already smell the death that surrounds him."

"Will it be our deaths?"

"Could be," I said. "You ever fought Indians before?"

"Sir, I never even fired a gun in anger. I was an artillery instructor at West Point."

"Then stay close to me," I said. "Stay with the wagons. They provide cover. Take your time. Never fire at a Sioux that's not coming at you. Wait for him to close, then fire. And use your pistol, not your saber. The Sioux can outfight any man alive hand to hand."

We sat down outside the tent for a while talking about Washington and Baltimore. Then the darkness all around us was shattered by a flash of lightning. In the distance, the rumble of thunder found our ears.

"Have you ever thought about dying?" he asked me.

"Not much," I said. "The Indians believe the world begins and ends with a man's life. I'm too much of a white man not to think to the future, though. I have a son and a daughter to raise. But I know that what happens will come no matter what I think. A man lives and dies. The time and place of neither is a man's own choice."

"What about the Indians? Are they afraid of death?"

"The Sioux are afraid only of defeat."

"Then they'll fight until they die?"

"They've been dying since the white man first came into their lands. Death is sometimes easier than living. When it becomes that way, you have an enemy that's totally fearless.

He's like a wounded animal. If he's going to die, he's going to strike you down, too."

"Is their attack terrible?"

"Yes," I said. "But no more terrible than a company of cavalry riding down on a Sioux village. It's the nature of war to be terrible. Death is terrible."

We warmed our hands by the campfire as the night settled in. Then Captain Talbot joined us.

"Well, Whitlock," he said, "you seem to feel the Sioux have found us."

"Nothing moves in this valley that they don't see. Even a blind man could smell your cooking fires. If Twisted Nose wishes to kill white men, then he will find many tomorrow to kill," I told him.

"And you would ride out and seek him?" the captain asked.

"I would go to him. I wear a necklace given to me by a Sioux warrior. There are those who may remember me. They would trust my words," I explained, staring at his cold eyes.

"And when they see our men, our bright new rifles?" Captain Talbot asked me.

"When Twisted Nose sees your bright new rifles, he'll smile. The Sioux can kill many white men with new rifles taken from dead soldiers."

"You don't give us much of a chance, do you?" the captain asked.

"Send me out ahead with a good sergeant, one who knows the country. Then put out flank riders. If you ride out in column, the Sioux will cut you to pieces."

"Well, Whitlock," Captain Talbot said, "I've fought and killed a lot of Sioux and Cheyenne in my time. We'll ride out and meet Twisted Nose, and it will be him that gets buried."

"I wish you luck," I said. "You will need it."

"Will you ride at my side?" the captain asked me.

"I'll ride where I'm told to. My father was a soldier, and I understand how to follow orders," I said. "I'll die at your side. It would be a brave death."

"You're afraid?" the captain asked.

"No," I said. "But I know the signs of the mountains, and there's no sign of victory for us in the morning. We must win in time, but the battle you ask for can only end in death and defeat. I can fight and die as well as any man."

"That's what I hoped you'd say," Captain Talbot said. "My plan is to draw Twisted Nose out into an attack. I'll need someone to stay with the wagons. You can help the lieutenant guard them."

I looked at him stone-faced. The lieutenant's eyes glowed with the news that he'd have someone there to depend on, but I read the captain's thoughts. The wagons would be sacrificed so that the cavalry could have its share of the glory.

I slept that night in the tent as a gentle autumn rain fell outside. It was a restless night for me, and I could see that Lieutenant Hastings lay awake all night, too. The eve of battle was always a time of tension, a moment of trial for even the most tested of warriors. I wondered inside if Twisted Nose slept well. I thought not, for a man who rides to his death rarely fills his heart with peace.

CHAPTER 22

Morning comes early in the Powder River Valley, and it was
a bright yellow sun that greeted our eyes. I had slept lightly,
and the scurrying of the morning birds brought me to life.
I jumped to my feet and shook off the chill of the autumn
air. Then I got dressed and walked out of the tall army tent.

The camp was already stirring. The cooks were busy with
a hot breakfast, and small fires were blazing around the tents
of the enlisted men. I saw no officers, so I walked to the picket
line where the horses were tied.

Corporal Griffiths paced in front of the army mounts, and
I nodded to him as I stroked the big sorrel's nose.

Soon the soldiers broke camp and packed the wagons. I
watched the looks that came to their eyes. The young men
were bewildered. They followed their orders in a confused
manner, trying to move as fast as the sergeants told them. The
handful of veterans frowned and looked uncomfortable. They
busied themselves cleaning their guns, tending their horses,
grabbing an extra box of cartridges for their Winchesters.

As busy as the veterans kept themselves, I could tell they
all had one thing in common. They were scared. And not a
man among them looked as if he expected to ride out of the
Powder River Valley again.

Before the sun had climbed to the treetops, we were in
motion. Captain Talbot led our long column, his brass buttons
shining in the sunlight. Behind him came the soldiers in a
perfect column of twos. The men looked grim, determined.
They meant to make the Sioux pay for the death that would
come.

I rode with Lieutenant Hastings and four other troopers behind the wagons. I wore the thick bearskin coat around my shoulders, hoping it might give some protection from a Sioux war lance or knife. But there was no shield known to man that could stave off a bullet fired accurately by a determined enemy. And there was no more determined enemy than a Sioux warrior who knew his world had no more tomorrows.

As Crazy Woman Creek disappeared into the mountains behind us, a strange feeling worked its way down my spine. It was as if we were being watched, scouted, examined. But the eyes I felt on my back were cold eyes, eyes that did not belong to the living. I felt as if the spirits of the mountains were watching.

The others grew uneasy, too. A shudder seemed to wind its way through the entire column. I heard horses stir, too, and words whispered through the trees. Then I saw what it was. On the side of a mountain ahead of us was a large Sioux burial ground. As we rode on, I realized what was chilling my soul. There were fresh scaffolds in the burial ground. The warriors whose bones rested there were not long dead.

I pulled my horse out of the column and rode forward. When I reached the vanguard of the column, I hailed Captain Talbot.

"Captain Talbot," I said. "You have to disperse the men."

"Whitlock, get back to the wagons," the captain ordered.

"Don't you have eyes?" I asked him. "Look on the mountain. You've just ridden past a Sioux burial ground. Can't you tell the difference between fresh scaffolds and old ones?"

"Are you sure?" he asked.

"I know the Sioux, and I know wood. I can tell what's been cut recently. Twisted Nose can't be far from here."

"Getting nervous?" he asked with a cruel smile.

"I'm not in a hurry to die," I said. "You must know the Sioux camps are close. Twisted Nose can't let you get close to his camps. He'll attack soon."

"Do you know of a place where the Sioux might camp near here? Could you lead us there?"

"There are places," I said. "But to reach any of them would be to expose your whole force to attack. At least on the road, Twisted Nose can only attack one end at a time. In the broken country you'd have to ride through, those green troops of yours would be picked off like flies."

"And what would you do?"

"Send a man ahead to scout the land. Let me try to talk Twisted Nose into coming peacefully back to the fort."

"You must be a Sioux," the captain said, laughing. "You live on dreams. The Army doesn't want the Sioux at Fort Fetterman. The Army wants the Sioux dead."

"But what about Colonel Masterson?"

"There are always a few colonels, a few privates, a few senators who have bleeding hearts. But Sheridan is the man who counts, and he has no love for Indians."

I looked at him with the same grim face the soldiers wore.

"Then I'll go back to my place," I said. "It seems like this would be a good moment to plan my last battle."

I rode back to the wagons and pulled the sorrel into line with Lieutenant Hastings.

"Did you warn the captain?" Lieutenant Hastings asked.

"The captain didn't want a warning," I said. "The captain only wants to die."

"And us?"

"There will be many graves in this valley," I said sadly. "A few may get away, but most of us will die. I hear the spirits of the night. They tell me that the land I came in search of is no more. I'm lost. It's not really so much more difficult to die than to be lost."

"But you have a family," the lieutenant reminded me.

"What good am I to them?" I asked. "I don't know what I can do for someone else when I can't do anything for myself."

We rode on, listening to the stirring of the leaves and the hooting of the owls. Those of us who'd been in the land of the Sioux before recognized the sounds of the Sioux scouts, the soft step of their unshod ponies on the hillside.

As we wound our way around the side of the mountain, a

terrible shriek broke the stillness. The shriek was followed by a series of war cries and shouts from the mountainside above us. Then a wave of bare-chested Sioux warriors hit the column in front of us.

I had no time for thinking now. Lieutenant Hastings stared at the confusion ahead of us, and I galloped ahead to get the wagons into a defensive position.

"Form a circle," I shouted to the sergeant in charge of the teamsters. "Get the horses in the center. Try to form a line."

I'd never served an hour in the Army, but I'd seen close up the actions of fine commanders since childhood. Some of the soldiers looked at me with surprise or confusion, but the sergeant did as I said. Sergeants recognized the firmness of command more than the authority of rank.

Up ahead the column was disintegrating. Inexperienced soldiers dismounted their horses and ran into the trees. Their death cries were horrifying.

I watched two young lieutenants struck down by war lances, and I realized the center of our force was lost. The troopers fired in desperation at the phantom Sioux, but the Indians were moving in every direction at once, striking all the while. And blue-coated soldiers were falling like Maryland wheat.

I started to ride out to the soldiers, but I heard my name shouted from behind me. I turned to see Lieutenant Hastings calling for me, his eyes frozen in terror. I turned and rode to him.

"Mr. Whitlock, what do we do?" the lieutenant asked me.

I glanced around at our little force. Besides the lieutenant and myself, we had about seventeen soldiers, half of whom had scrambled to the wagons after losing their horses in the melee in front of us.

"Keep the horses inside the circle of wagons," I told him. "Then take cover and make a stand."

"A last stand," one of the soldiers said.

"If this is the time for us to die," I said softly, "then we can at least see to it that the Sioux who kill us remember we were warriors."

The others looked at me strangely. I understood how they felt. They didn't ride out there by choice. All they wanted was to return to their homes, their loved ones. I had accepted death.

"Dismount!" Lieutenant Hastings commanded. "Get the horses inside the wagons!"

The soldiers led their horses between the wagons into the open area inside their protective circle. Then they crawled underneath wagons or hid inside them. I braced my rifle on a wagon tongue and set my sights on a young Sioux. I fired, and death covered his eyes. Johnny Cougar Claw, who had come to the mountains to save the Sioux, was now taking part in the ending of that tribe.

The battle continued beyond our eyesight. Death and smoke filled the valley ahead of us, but we didn't have time to worry about the others. The Sioux formed in a clearing ahead of us and charged our position.

I set my sights on a painted warrior wearing a wolf's head over his face. I blew him out of the saddle, but the Sioux charge did not falter. It swept through the wagons, and most of the soldiers were cut down. I turned in time to see Lieutenant Hastings strike a Sioux in the shoulder with his saber. Then the Sioux flashed a knife and opened up the young lieutenant's belly.

A sadness came to my heart when I saw the lieutenant stagger backward. Then the Sioux flashed the knife again, and darkness clouded the eyes of the lieutenant.

I found myself surrounded by Sioux now. I blocked one man away with my rifle. A second broke through from behind me, but I shot him with my pistol. Then I reached for my knife and leaped on a third warrior.

As I plunged my knife into the side of the Sioux, he cut a great gash in my left thigh. I fell backward, rolling beside one of the wagons. Then I looked above me at a grim-faced warrior wearing the war bonnet of a chief. His nose was shattered, and his eyes were filled by a great hatred. I watched him fall on me with a war club in his hand.

I blocked the war club away with my left hand, then turned the chief around. But he tore the knife from my hand and pinned me to the earth. I watched him hold his knife high in the air so that the sun flashed brightly off its blade. Then he tore open my shirt and prepared to end my life.

I accepted this death for it was the brave one I sought. Death in battle at the hands of a chief was an end that might be sung of around campfires. But as I looked into his eyes in my moment of death, I saw a tremble come to his lips. His eyes softened, and he plunged his knife into the ground beside my face.

He looked intently into my eyes. Then he clasped my shoulders firmly in his hands and slung me over his shoulder. As I was carried into the trees, I saw that around the chief's neck hung a necklace of eight cougar claws.

I had come into the mountains in search of my lost brother, the other part of me that had always understood. In the moment of our deaths, we had suddenly come together once more. Twisted Nose was none other than that brother, Antelope Foot.

If he had been a white man, he would have taken my life that very moment. But there is an honor among the Sioux that remembers what was, that waits to understand what is before killing. I knew I would have my chance to speak with the chief Captain Talbot knew as Twisted Nose. And then there would be a moment of living or dying.

Antelope Foot, for as such I would always know him, carried me to a riderless pony. He helped me onto the horse, pausing only to bind the gash in my thigh. Then he gave the pony's rope to another warrior and rode away to rejoin the battle. With him went my fate.

CHAPTER 23

Nightfall found me alone on the mountainside above the Sioux camp. It was a silent camp, and there were no fires. I saw only a few women, and no children ran through the fires as they did when I slept among the Sioux as a boy. I saw the sign of death upon that camp, the same sign I felt marked my heart.

As I sat in the silence of the mountains, I remembered the hundreds of times I'd shared Antelope Foot's campfire with him. I remembered the killing of the cougar, the buffalo hunt, the night we stood together and spoke of the death of his father. And now we had come to bring each other's deaths.

I looked to the base of the mountain. No guard kept watch over me. At my feet lay my rifle and the old painted knife Black Kettle had given me. The Sioux offered me a choice. I could leave if that was my choice, or I could stay and explain myself.

I knew that if Antelope Foot could not kill me after I had taken the lives of his brothers, then I couldn't walk away into the darkness without speaking with him. For whatever it was worth, there remained a bond between us.

As the moon rose above the valley, the stillness was split by a haunting war cry. Into the camp rode fifteen riders leading two wagons and some thirty army horses. Leading them was their chief, Twisted Nose.

But Twisted Nose did not stay in the camp. He rode to the mountainside below me. Looking up at me, he put on a grim face. Then he stepped down from his horse and walked to where my rifle was laying. He placed his own rifle and two knives beside my own. Then he made his way to me and sat down beside me.

"You have been long gone from the mountains, Cougar Claw," he said to me.

"My heart has never left this place," I told him. "I have been to the other world, but it had no place for me."

"Why do you ride with the long knife?" he asked. "You kill Sioux, Cougar Claw. Do you not remember the nights you slept in our camps? Do you not remember the summers we camped together? Your journey into the other world has left you a man without memory."

"I remember everything that's ever happened," I told him. "If I was the man you speak of now, I would not be here. You own my life, my brother. I see before me Antelope Foot, son of Painted Bow. I see before me the man who grew from the boy who ran with me through the summers of my youth. I see anger in your eyes, but there is no anger in my heart."

"But the long knife rides with anger in his eyes," he said to me. "We watch many hours the line of soldiers. You ride to the long knife chief to warn him of us."

"Yes," I said. "But he would not stop. He knew what I didn't. Even in his defeat he's killed you. I see in your camp the signs of death. No children run through the fires. No women cry for the dead. The captain has emptied your ponies of their riders. Now the wagons will roll on through the last home of the Sioux."

"This you have brought with you, Cougar Claw," he said.

"This I have tried to stop," I objected. "The eagle chief at Laramie asked me to ride to you. He spoke to me of the last chief of the Sioux who would not surrender. This man he called Twisted Nose. He said to me that I should ride into the mountains to seek you out. I should tell you that there is only death in the mountains. I should speak to you of riding out of the mountains, leaving the old places."

"To leave the places of our people is to bring the death of the old ways," he said. "I will die here before I will lose the old ways."

"But if you die, the old ways die with you. Who will tell your sons of the old ways?"

"I have no sons," he said bitterly. "Those who rode beside me, those I held in my hands on the day of their birth are no more. They lie on the mountain with their mother, killed by the long knife in their lodge. They died, as my father died, at the hand of the white man."

I looked at my feet. I could say nothing. Finally I looked into the sorrow that filled his eyes.

"Antelope Foot, my brother, I mourn their passing, though I never shared their laughter, never knew their smiles. I have a son in the East I barely know. I have a daughter who is the joy of my world."

"You would ride to your death here with children in the other world, Cougar Claw? This is not the way of the mountains."

"I hoped to find the heart I lost in my journey," I said. "A man is no use to his son if he is not a man. The world in the East has no room for men. It is a land of wolves. I would have my son know the mountains, fish the rivers, hunt the buffalo in the valleys we have walked in friendship. But to be a father to my son, I must find my brother and know that I'm still the man I once was."

"Are you the man who once called me brother?" he asked. "I am not the same man I was. You call me Antelope Foot. The boy who was called Antelope Foot is no more. I am Twisted Nose. I earn my name when I kill six long knife on the Rosebud. I am dead to life. I only wait upon my death."

"You speak as Twisted Nose, my brother, but the eyes I see are those of Antelope Foot. I speak to you as Cougar Claw. Are not the eyes you see those you remember from the nights we shared in the summers of our youth?"

"This is so," he said. "But the times have changed. I can speak to you only of how death comes to the Sioux. I can speak only of sadness."

"It seems strange to me, my brother, that the man who has

taught me so much of life should now speak to me only of death."

"This is a time of dying," he said.

"But for me it's a time of being born," I said. "When you held your knife away from my heart, you gave me birth from the mountain spirit inside you. If you had forgotten all that is within me, all that binds us together, you would not have stayed your hand."

"A Sioux remembers always," he told me. "The claws of the cougar bind us together to the time that one releases the other."

"It was never my wish to bind you to something by my action," I said. "I always felt in my heart a bond to you. I wouldn't have you bound to me except by your own desire. If you ask release, you have it."

"Cougar Claw," he said, running his fingers over the jagged scars on my chest. "You are forever marked by what has been. Your heart is not changed. But this place no longer belong to you and me. It belong to past. For us there is nothing. We only walk the mountains now in search of death."

"I wait for mine," I said. "Your knife is beside you."

"This is not the moment," he said. "Tell me this, Cougar Claw. You come to this place to find your heart. Do you find this heart of yours?"

"I have found it," I said. "I'm at peace with what I am."

"This is great thing. In another time we would have sung many songs of this. But it is not another time. The thunder which lights the heavens tells me that the winter snows will soon come. This will be a winter cold with death. We would once have slept warm in our lodges, eager for the coming of summer. But there will be no summer rain for the Sioux. Only the snows of winter and the death which follows. You, my brother, will see the gentle thunder of summer once more. You will walk the buffalo valleys with your son. You will sing to him of the old ways. You will sing to him of your brother's death. You will remember the man who gave you your life?"

"You would give me my life?"

"You once spared my life when it was in your hands to take it. You gave me the life which I hold now, and the lives of others. The lives you took this morning weigh heavy on my mind, but a man who has spared a life must have his payment."

"You give me my life, but you will not take your own. This is not right."

"This is as it must be, Cougar Claw. Once the mountains echoed with the songs of the Sioux. Once the buffalo valleys shook at the thunder of our ponies. Once the white man trembled at the sight of our war chiefs. But these days are gone.

"My sons and I rode proudly the mountains. But they are dead now, as are my fathers. The Sioux once were the great hunters of the lands. Now they are like buffalo, all gone. Those of us who live still are hunted like game, for the sport of the white man.

"I will never leave this place, Cougar Claw. There are few of us left, but this is the life I was born to, and this is the place I will die. I can do no other but to stay. I can be no other than that which I am."

"If you stay, they will come and kill you. Death is never something a man should seek, my brother. Life is always better than death."

"No, Cougar Claw. Life is pain. I do not seek my death, but I will not run from it. My death has been written in the clouds of many sunsets. But it will not be a bad death. It will be proud. I have seen it in many dreams. I will stand tall on the mountain with my war lance in my hand. Behind me will be the place where the bones of my sons rest. There I will be struck down in the final hour of the Sioux nation."

"It is a brave death," I said. "But there is no victory in it. There is no courage in the taking of your life. It must be a coward who strikes you down."

"No, my brother. It will be the bravest of all men who brings my death. It will be a man with a heart of the mountains, like myself. No great warrior can fall at the hands of a coward."

"You're talking of the old ways," I said. "Now the men who come to the mountains are from the East. They are wolves preying on the flesh of their brothers. They are mostly cowards."

"But when my dreams speak to me, Cougar Claw, they come to be as I see them. I have seen many things, and they have come to be."

"And did you see me?" I asked.

"This I must not speak of, Cougar Claw. My spirit holds these things for my eyes alone. To speak of what will come to you is not to be. You must seek your own answers."

"So what is to become of us, my brother? You will stay here to die. Am I to ride away and find life?"

"It was always meant to be this way, Cougar Claw. Even when we ran against each other as boys, it was you who won. You were the one who killed the cougar. You were the one who was marked for life, even in the moment of death."

"Only because you granted me life," I said. "You say that I saved your life, but that was not the truth. I killed the cougar, but you bound my wounds. I chose not to take your life in the other war, but you spared me this morning. If we are still bound, it is a binding by the ropes of life and love. It is a spirit which walks our hearts which binds us."

"Yes, Cougar Claw, this will always be. But you will be visited by great pain because of what you say."

"I know pain well," I told him. "Pain is an old companion of mine."

"Would you take to my lodge this last night of my life?" he asked me. "Would you share with me the meat of the last deer I will kill?"

"Why not?" I asked him. "We shared the meat of the first deer I killed."

His eyes lit up with the recollection, and I felt his hand on my shoulder. We stumbled to our feet and looked at the guns and knives on the ground in front of us. We walked past them and made our way to the camp below.

That night we ate and laughed and remembered. I felt the

cold stares and hatred of the other Sioux, but I didn't try to explain to them. They could never understand the times we had shared, and it wouldn't matter tomorrow. They all had the mark of death in their eyes.

I slept that night alone on the mountain overlooking the Sioux village. I felt the world closing in on me, and I knew I would never again walk the valleys with my brother, be his name Antelope Foot or Twisted Nose. I would be on my way back to Laramie tomorrow, and the Sioux would await their deaths.

CHAPTER 24

The sun has a way of restoring life to the weary. As daylight broke over the valley, I stirred into life. I walked over and picked up my knife. Then I put it in the scabbard on my boot. Next I picked up my Winchester and rubbed the barrel with my coat to remove the moisture. Then I looked at the camp of the Sioux below me.

There was not a sign of life there. No guards had been posted. No fires burned. It was a village of death. The Sioux were not even defending themselves.

There was nothing bright about the morning. Heavy black clouds rolled in from the northwest, and there was a roll of thunder through the heavens.

"Angry thunder," I mumbled to myself.

It was fitting that the skies would be alive with violent thunder on the day a proud people would cease to be. I felt as if the spirits of the sky were protesting against what was to happen.

I picked up a handful of dirt and let it drop through my fingers. It was as much as I would ever have of the mountains, but they would always own me. It seemed unfair.

I walked down from the mountain, knowing I walked into a day I'd never sought, a day I'd always feared above all things. The heavy dew clung to me, bringing a damp chill to my bones. I walked with heavy steps, the jagged wound in my thigh burning with pain. When I approached the village, a young Sioux warrior stepped out and stopped me.

"Have you not sought the death of our people, white man?" he asked me in the tongue of the Sioux. "Go from this place."

"I would speak this last time to my brother, Twisted Nose," I said to him.

"Twisted Nose is no brother to the white man," the Sioux said. "Our men sing songs of the death he has brought to the white man. Many white women cry for their dead because of our chief."

"Tell him I wait for him," I said, sitting quietly outside the tepee.

The young Sioux walked over to the lodge of his chief and went inside to tell him I was there. A short while later Twisted Nose stepped out into the morning, his chest bare and painted for war.

"Why do you come to me on the morning of my death?" he asked. "Why are you not gone from this place, Cougar Claw?"

"Can you not hear the heavens?" I asked him. "The spirits of the mountain cry out in anger that this death may not come."

"You read the skies well, my brother," Twisted Nose said to me, the hatred in his eyes softening with the memory of the old times. "But the anger is not for me."

"It's for me, then," I said, frowning.

"No, my brother," Twisted Nose said, placing his strong hand on my shoulder. "It is anger at the white man. It is anger for a hundred broken promises, a hundred broken treaties. It is anger for a thousand lies, a thousand deaths. It is anger born from the old ways that would not die quietly as in the sleep of old age. It is an anger that is shared by your heart, an anger which walks in your eyes."

"But this cannot be the place of your death," I said. "Your dream spoke not of a valley. You must die on the mountain."

"I will fall on the mountain, Cougar Claw, the last of my people. My hand will be the last raised in anger."

"But Twisted Nose, many Sioux live with Red Cloud in the Dakotas. Red Cloud was a great chief. Could you not go to him?"

"Red Cloud read the end of our ways," Twisted Nose said. "He would live to see a sunrise born of a new life. I have not the heart for the new world he waits upon. I will die with the old one."

"Then this is the last time we speak," I said to him. "I give you my hand in friendship. I will mourn your death, my brother."

I took his hand in mine, and the power in our arms bound us together as in the days of our youth.

"Speak of me to your sons," Twisted Nose said.

I looked at him a last time. Then I walked away.

"Cougar Claw," he called to me, "there are many ponies in this camp. Take one that suits you. Your leg burns with fever. To walk is death for you."

"Yes," I said, walking to where the horses were tied. "I go with the peace which should always have filled this land."

"Yes, my brother," Twisted Nose told me.

I found a strong young mustang and climbed on its back. Then I waved a last good-by to my friend and rode off down the valley.

Every foot I traveled brought new pain to my leg. When I passed out of sight of the Sioux camp, I led the mustang over into some trees and dismounted. After tying the horse to a pine tree, I tore away the binding Twisted Nose had put on my thigh.

The wound was already alive with dark fluids. I leaned back on a rock and remembered what Trader Jim had taught me about wounds. I put my hands on opposite sides of my leg and pulled the wound open.

Pus oozed from the wound, but as it drained, the swelling lessened, and the pain grew lighter. I took some herb mixture from a small pouch on my belt and sprinkled it into the gash. Then I tore strips from my cotton shirt and rebound the wound.

As I sat among the trees, I heard a strange noise in my ears. It sounded like a band. I thought for a moment my mind was playing tricks on me, but then I saw where the noise came from. A long column of bright blue uniforms rode into the valley led by a tall officer in the uniform of a colonel. Behind him rode soldiers playing a strange melody with trumpets and fifes.

The idea of a detachment of cavalry riding down the last Sioux warriors to the sound of a regimental band tore at me. I shook off the pain in my leg and got to my feet. Then I slung my weary body over the back of the mustang and rode out to meet the cavalry.

I held my arm up to greet the colonel, watching a dozen rifle barrels leveled in my direction.

"I come in peace," I said to him, stopping my horse away from the column.

Two young corporals rode out to bring me in, their eyes filled with suspicion. They led me to the colonel, whose heavy black eyebrows and bushy beard gave him the look of some biblical warrior.

"I'm John Whitlock," I said. "I rode from Fort Fetterman with a cavalry troop under the command of Captain Talbot. We were cut to pieces by a Sioux attack."

"We came across Captain Talbot's men yesterday," the colonel said. "Why are you so far from them?"

"I was taken by the Sioux," I told him. "I was in the rear with the wagons. We put up a stiff fight, but we never had a chance."

"Then why did the Sioux let you go?" a captain asked. "Captain Talbot had three arrows and a lance in him. Some of the men who survived were cut up pretty bad."

"I have a gash in my leg," I said, pointing to the wound in my thigh. "But I know the Sioux. I hunted with them as a boy. The warrior who took me remembered me. I saved his life once, and he let me go."

"This all sounds like a fairy tale," one of the officers said. "I believe this man should be held with the supply train."

"That's no saber wound on his thigh," the colonel said. "I fought at Manassas with a Whitlock."

"My father, sir," I said.

"If you're John Whitlock's boy, then you're no traitor," the

colonel told me. "I'm Colonel Jubal McDonald. We're trying
to find the Sioux camps."

"If you've sent out scouts, they must have told you you're
nearly on top of the Sioux," I said.

"I hoped to hear it from you," the colonel said. "How are
the defenses set?"

"They aren't defending themselves," I said. "There aren't
but a handful of them left. They're just waiting for their
deaths."

"That doesn't sound like Twisted Nose," a captain said,
shaking his head. "Maybe this is some other band."

"Do you know Twisted Nose?" I asked him. "Have you
spoken to him?"

"I've had his bullets taken out of my hide," the captain said.
"I've chased him through these mountains since the Little
Bighorn."

"But you still don't know him," I said. "He will die here
this day. He will never leave. This very morning he stands in
the valley waiting for you."

"How many men does he have with him?" the colonel
asked.

"All that are left," I said. "Only a handful, and some are
only boys. The rest are dead."

"You know this Twisted Nose pretty well, do you?" the captain asked me.

"I hunted with him in these very mountains when I was a
boy," I told them. "He was at my side when I killed my first
deer. I stood beside him at his father's funeral. Have you seen
the necklace of cougar claws he wears around his neck?"

"Many times," the captain said.

"Look then at mine," I said, holding it away from my
throat.

The men looked at me with both surprise and suspicion.
For several minutes the valley was filled with silence. Then
the colonel smiled.

"Would you ride with us, Whitlock?" Colonel McDonald
asked me.

"I'll ride with you to the camp," I said. "But I'll not ride against the Sioux. I have too many deaths on my hands already."

"Then ride back with the artillery," the colonel said.

I turned the mustang and rode back to the big guns. As my eyes looked at the long barrels of the cannons, I knew there was no tomorrow for the Sioux.

The army of blue-coated soldiers filled the valley with their numbers. The colonel formed up his men in two columns with the artillery in the center. Then the band began playing, and the guns opened up with great blasts of thunder.

It seemed to me that the thunder of the skies echoed the thunder of the big guns, and the valley filled with a terrible din. Then the cavalry charged, and the Sioux stepped forward to meet them.

Even the women and little children among the Sioux held lances or rifles. They waited for the long knives of the soldiers to cut them down. I watched with a mournful heart as one after another the Sioux warriors fell.

One boy about twelve years old fought at the side of Twisted Nose. That boy would not let the soldiers past him. Three times sabers cut through the fragile fabric of the boy's body, but it was as if the spirit of the mountains would not let the life leave this boy.

I thought to myself that the boy stood where I should have fought. But it was not to be that way, and I knew the difference that had been between us since the day of our births kept us apart at the moment of his death.

The soldiers charged again the thin line of Sioux warriors, and this time there was no resisting. A fourth saber flashed across the boy's face, and Twisted Nose stood alone. The other Sioux died bravely one by one. As the last of Twisted Nose's men fell into the silence of eternal sleep, the chief gave out a loud cry.

It was answered by the skies. Lightning flashed in a dozen directions, and the clouds emptied. Rain fell all around us, and Twisted Nose made a rush for a cavalry mount. In a second the chief was mounted. Twisted Nose then cut down two soldiers and rode out in front of the artillery. He flashed his angry eyes over the valley and cried out in fury. Then Twisted Nose, the last of the Sioux warriors, rode into the rain and vanished from sight.

CHAPTER 25

The carnage that remains after a battle is terrible to behold. The hacked and dismembered bodies of the dead litter the field. Discarded weapons are scattered where their former owners left them. Riderless horses haunt the field with their eerie groans. And worst of all are the anguished cries of the wounded.

The remains of the Indian camp were being taken apart by the surviving cavalrymen. The dead Sioux were stripped of necklaces, bracelets, battle dress, anything of interest or value. I stood over the dead body of the Sioux boy. I cried inside my heart as I saw his slashed body and youthful face. Then I moved aside as a soldier came to take the boy's moccasins.

"For my kid," the soldier said.

"You don't mind, do you, boy?" I whispered to the dead boy. "They will serve you no longer."

The soldiers finished stripping the bodies of the dead. Then they burned the tepees after carrying away every blanket and buffalo hide that could be collected. I felt a hand on my shoulder as I tried to turn away from the scene.

"Would you let me see to that leg, young man?" an officer carrying a medical case asked me. "It appears to me you're working up to a mighty fine infection."

"Thank you," I said to him, following the doctor to the little improvised field hospital he'd set up.

The doctor washed the wound and dressed it with clean cotton bandages. I felt the pain inside my leg pass away from me when he finished.

"I'll see what we can do about getting you a pair of trousers and a new shirt," the doctor said. "We've got loads of supplies. I'm sure the colonel can muster something together for the son of an old friend."

"Thank you," I said, trying to manage a smile.

I watched the pain on the faces of the other wounded soldiers. Most of them were young, and many would not last the night. I wondered why of all the men who'd taken the field I had been destined to live. But the mountains have strange ways, and it is not a man's way to question the spirits.

I remembered what Twisted Nose had said the night before. The cougar had marked me as the one who would live. It was a burden I would bear with me forever.

A young private walked over and presented me with the uniform trousers of an officer. He also handed me a shirt. I discarded the torn and bloody buckskin trousers and dressed myself. Then I shook the wetness out of my bearskin coat.

The sky had cleared now, and a perfect afternoon was upon us. The soldiers busied themselves with burial details while I tried to say some encouraging words to the dying men. Then I was called away by the colonel.

"Whitlock, might I have a word with you?" the colonel asked.

"Yes, sir," I said. "I'd like to thank you for the clothes."

"You're welcome to them," he said. "You said that you know this Twisted Nose. Could you come with me to look over the dead Indians? I have to identify them."

"Certainly," I said, following him to where the dead lay.

The Sioux lay face up side by side. The women were on one side, the men on the other. I walked along the line, looking at the naked bodies. The courage that had filled those men and women was nowhere to be seen now. The thing which came to my mind was that now they were only so many men and women, killed by their fellow men. Even the face of the brave boy was now filled only with death. As I spoke the names of those I knew, many memories filled my heart.

"But which one is Twisted Nose?" the colonel asked.

"Didn't you see Twisted Nose?" I asked him. "He came out

to taunt your men. When the others were killed, he rode away."

"Away?" the colonel said, shaking with rage. "That can't be. No one got away."

"He did," I said.

"This is a bad business," Colonel McDonald said, frowning. "If we let Twisted Nose ride away, the Sioux will say he's truly a ghost. They'll escape from the reservation and ride out to join him."

"He didn't run away," I said. "It's just that he seeks his death elsewhere."

"Elsewhere? Do you know where he's ridden to?"

"Yes," I said sadly.

"Can you lead us there? Can you show us this place?"

"Yes," I said again.

"Will you?" the colonel asked.

"I wish I could say that I won't," I said. "I'd like to lead you away from this place. But Twisted Nose said this is the day of his death, and he'd rather die as a brave man in the place of his choosing than alone in the dark of night, the victim of some farmer."

"The Sioux do know how to die," the colonel said, a look of respect in his eyes.

"They know the true way to live, too," I said. "But no one left them alone to live their lives in their own way. The Sioux will be missed in these mountains."

"Yes," the colonel said, agreeing with me.

The colonel left a captain in charge of the burial detail. He left behind the big guns and the supply wagons. He took with us only twenty troopers, all veterans of many battles. Then we rode off down the valley.

I knew where Twisted Nose waited for us. His face came to my mind. He would be standing beside the funeral scaffolds of his sons, waiting for the charge which would end his life and his ways.

My heart was clouded with the gloom that would fill the valley when Twisted Nose was dead. I rode alongside the colonel, but I said nothing. The soldiers behind us laughed and joked about the battle that morning, but I shared none of their joy at the ending of the Sioux in the Powder River Valley.

It was close to dusk when we rode down the Bozeman Road near the burial ground. Dead horses and broken rifles and lances remained to remind me of the battle that had been fought there. The air filled with an unearthly feeling, and I looked upon the last resting place of the Sioux warrior I'd known since boyhood.

"He'll be waiting up there," I said, waving my hand up toward the burial ground. "He will stand beside the scaffolds which support the bones of his sons. There he will wait for you to call his death."

"Sergeant," the colonel said. "Pair off the men. We'll ride up in pairs. Don't take any chances. If you get a clear shot, blow that Indian to kingdom come. I don't want to lose another man in this valley."

"No," I said. "This has to be done, but not like that. Look into the eyes of your men. They smile at the idea of bringing this man's death. It must be done, but not like this. It can't be done with relish. He's the last of a kind. His life should be taken with reluctance, with a mourning heart."

"You're a strange man, Whitlock. What would you have me do, send my men up one at a time for him to kill? He won't just stand there and be struck down, you know. He'll curse us with his dying gasp."

"Let me do it," I told them.

"You?" the colonel asked. "You told me this man was your friend. He spared your life. And now you'd climb the mountain to kill him?"

"He's led a brave life. He's earned a brave death," I said, my face grim and determined. "In another life we might have fought shoulder to shoulder against a common foe. In this life, in this world, on this day it must be my fate to end his life."

"You won't help him escape?" the colonel asked.

"He won't run," I said. "This is the place where he'll die. He's known it for many days."

"Then go," the colonel said. "But if he's still alive in half an hour, then we're coming up there to kill him."

"It won't take long," I said.

I slipped down off my horse and walked up the face of the mountain. As I came upon the fresh scaffolds, I saw him at last.

He stood in the chill autumn air naked except for a painted breechclout around his loins. His arms and legs and chest and face were all brightly painted in reds and yellows, the colors of the earth. Around his neck was the necklace of cougar claws.

"I knew this would be the place," I said. "I felt it when I passed it the first time yesterday. There was something strange calling to me here."

"I have seen it many times in my dreams," he told me.

"But you didn't say it would be me that brought your death," I said to him. "You didn't speak of that."

"It was not the time, my brother. Yesterday, even this morning, was another life. Tell me, Cougar Claw, why did you come to me now? You could have left this to the soldiers."

"You told me that you would die this day. You said you wished a brave death. The soldiers could not have brought you such a death. I understand what must be done."

"Can you do this, Cougar Claw? You are weak from the wound in your leg. You have not the heart for killing me."

"I can do what I must," I said.

"You will prepare a place for my bones? You will not let the long knife pick at my body?"

"I will tend to you in the way of your fathers," I said. "You will rest here among the spirits of your fathers, beside the bones of your sons."

"Then all is well, my brother," he told me.

Twisted Nose then stepped away from the scaffolds and took out his war lance. He watched the look on my face. Then his eyes turned dark with a coldness I'd never seen. I knew at that moment that he intended to make the taking of his life no easy thing.

He cried out in a great terrible yell. Then he came at me with the lance.

I would have liked to take his life with a war lance. I would like for him to have died in the old fashion. But the look in his eyes chilled my soul, and I took out my revolver. Then I fired twice, sending the bullets that killed him into his head.

His eyes froze with a sudden stillness, and the lance fell from his hands. Then he sank to his knees, and his face was covered by a shadow of death. As his eyes grew black with death, his lips whispered softly the death chant of the Sioux. And then he was no more.

The soldiers rode into our presence, stopping as they saw the figure of Twisted Nose lying dead at my feet. One of them walked to us and bent over him.

"Leave him alone!" I shouted. "Don't touch his body!"

The sergeant then bellowed for the soldiers to stand clear. As I cradled the head of my dead friend in my lap, the colonel rode beside us.

"Is this Twisted Nose?" he asked.

"He was known to you as Twisted Nose," I said, tears forming in my eyes. "I ran with this man as a boy through the summers of my youth."

"I'll get some men to bury him," the colonel said.

"No," I told him. "I will tend him. Please leave me alone with him."

"I can't leave you alone in this place, wounded and without shelter," the colonel objected.

"I'm all right," I said. "I'm used to the mountains. There are things which must be done. I'll return in my own time."

"Good luck, son," the colonel said. "You're worthy of a great friend. Men like you will be needed if the West is to remain strong."

I turned from the soldiers as they rode away. Then I walked into the woods to cut the timber for the burial scaffold of my friend, my brother, the boy I knew as Antelope Foot. Here would rest the bones of the great warrior who brought fear to the hearts of his enemies as the war chief of the Sioux, Twisted Nose.

CHAPTER 26

A warrior's funeral should always take place just as the sun goes down. But by the time I had the scaffold erected, the sun had been gone many hours. I knew the soul of my brother had passed from this world already, and so I waited for the sun to rise to say my words to his spirit.

The morning came early. The sun was unusually bright for the autumn, basking the valley in a golden glow that should have been saved for springtime. I thought that his funeral should have been at twilight, symbolizing the passing of a way of life. But the funeral was as much for me as it was for him, and perhaps the dawn held forth a new beginning for me and the land.

I wrapped his body in a painted Sioux blanket I took from his horse. Beside him I laid his war lance and his rifle, his knife and his bow. On his head I placed the great war bonnet he'd worn in battle. The necklace of cougar claws still hung from around his neck, but I took from my own neck the old necklace of silver he'd given me ten years before. I sadly put the silver necklace back around his neck where it had once hung.

I sat down at the foot of his scaffold and sang softly an old Sioux song I'd learned in my childhood. I'd never understood its meaning, but it seemed the right time for old songs. When I finished, I stood up.

"Spirit of the mountains, hold this friend, this brother of mine. He was known to you. Keep him close to your heart."

I walked to my horse and climbed on its back. Then I rode

out onto the Bozeman Road headed for the Platte and a new
life in a different kind of world.

The world changes. The people who walked with me the
world of my youth had all died. Even the sky seemed frozen
in stillness. The thunder's angry cry, like that of the Sioux,
had been silenced. The voices of truth and honor spoke no
longer.

A man can stand tall only as long as the spirits hold back
the onslaught of time. Even the courage of a man offers no
protection from what is destined to be. But often it seems a
wise man can find in a brave and defiant death a victory over
life.

I remembered something an old Cheyenne had told me in
my boyhood. Only the stars and the earth are forever. All else
is bound to change. All men must die. It was a great truth.

I could not cry for the passing of the Sioux. They had
known their days were numbered, and they had died with a
dignity worthy of a great people.

For myself, I would not die for many summers. If the mark
of life was upon my face, then I would try to face the future
with a courage born of my past.

There were new towns springing up from among the bones
of the great buffalo herds. What had been was yielding to
what would come.

Towns would need bankers. Just perhaps there would be
room for a different kind of man, one whose heart was of the
mountains but whose eyes could look to the future.

I looked forward to the days when I would ride into the
mountains with my sons to teach them the old ways. I longed
for the day when I would sing to them of my brothers, the
Sioux. I longed for the men they would grow to become, men
not of the other world beyond the great waters, but who
found that they belonged to the land and to the mountains,
men who found that they held a place in their lives for truth
and honor.